HUMAN BEGINNINGS

Also by Olivia Vlahos

AFRICAN BEGINNINGS

Illustrated by Kyuzo Tsugami

HUMAN BEGINNINGS

Olivia Vlahos

The Viking Press   *New York*

Viking Compass Edition
Issued in 1970 by The Viking Press, Inc.
625 Madison Avenue, New York, N.Y. 10022

Distributed in Canada by
The Macmillan Company of Canada Limited

SBN 670-38601-4 (hardbound)
SBN 670-38602-2 (library binding)
SBN 670-00279-8 (paperbound)

Library of Congress catalog card number: AC 66-10435

Printed in U.S.A.

ACKNOWLEDGMENTS

The idea for this book began in conversations with friends who shared with me a curiosity about the beginnings of things. In time and with study, the idea developed into a major project for the Master of Arts degree at Sarah Lawrence College. With the help of Professor Joseph Campbell it eventually became a book. From the very start, the intention has been to present in the clearest and simplest way possible the things scholars and specialists are discovering about man's beginnings. There are and doubtless always will be wide gaps separating known facts, gaps tentatively filled with theories and speculations—the educated guesses of scientists. I have wanted to include these as well.

A complete bibliography may be found at the end of the book. I should like, however, to express my indebtedness to those specialists on whose works I have leaned most heavily. They are: anthropologists Ralph Linton, William W. Howells, Loren Eiseley, Kenneth P. Oakley, L. S. B. Leakey, Carleton Coon, Irving Goldman; archaeologists Leonard Woolley, V. G. Childe, Robert

J. Braidwood; mythologist Joseph Campbell; linguists and specialists in linguistics Edward Sapir, Benjamin Whorf, Mario Pei; paleontologists Edwin H. Colbert, George Gaylord Simpson, Alfred Sherwood Romer, Elwyn L. Simons; physiologist Homer Smith; zoologist William Etkin.

Part One of the book has been read by Dr. Melissa L. Richter of the Natural Sciences Department of Sarah Lawrence College; Parts One and Two by Professor Irving Goldman of the Social Sciences Department and by Professor Campbell. All have been most generous with their time, their wisdom, and their interest, and I am very grateful. Their suggestions and criticisms have made this a better book than it might otherwise have been, and certainly they must not be held accountable for its shortcomings.

CONTENTS

PART TWO
BEING HUMAN

"Who are you? Name, please." Everyone is accustomed to such requests. And in one's own country, identification is not a very difficult task. The name is usually enough. Of course, if someone is being interviewed in an official way, a birth certificate or draft card or charge-plate might be required to prove that he is really the proprietor of the name in question. But in making a stranger's acquaintance, a simple introduction usually serves to start the conversational ball rolling. For there is a background of shared experiences—similar schools and similar foods, years of riding in similar cars, watching the same baseball games, and perhaps rooting for the same political party.

Suppose it is a foreigner who asks, "Who are you?" Let's make him a Frenchman or an Italian or a German or a Swede. In any language, your name alone will not now be enough to establish communication. Your questioner will have to get used to all sorts of peculiarly American things before he can truly understand *you*. Even with an interested Englishman you may have a bit of difficulty. You and he may have different words for the same things—his "lorry" and "petrol," for example, as against your "truck" and "gas." And there will be, of course, the bothersome business of idioms and expressions. Little mannerisms, perfectly acceptable to us, will seem to him quite shockingly rude.

With a visitor from the East the problems multiply. You will have to surmount religious differences, differences of attitude and personality and approach to life—even food taboos—before you can explain yourself and how you fit into your community and family and group.

If your questioner comes from a primitive society, you will be a total mystery. What does he care for your name when everything about you is so alien? The very clothes you wear, the house you live in, the car in the garage, even your haircut—all this strangeness blots *you* out of his picture. Still and all, understanding is not utterly impossible. You can always establish contact on an elementary *human* level. Let him make you a part of his family. Let him see you doing things he understands: helping, singing, hunting, caring for children. Let him put you in his frame of reference, and in time you can explain to him your own.

But wait. Suppose your questioner is not a foreigner, not a primitive. Suppose he is not even of this world—or this solar system. To make things really complicated, let's say he can't even talk the way you do. He communicates instead by beaming his thoughts directly into yours. Certainly he is an intelligent creature, but he is not human—not even remotely so. And when he asks, "Who are you? What are you?" the *what* is, to him, far more important than the *who*.

He needs to know how you came to look just the way you do. For your very hands and feet and eyes; the form of your body; your mouth and voice and the sounds they make—all these things will be to him great oddities. He will want to know what bearing your physical characteristics have on your thinking and just how complicated that thinking is. He will want to know in what ways you are like other living creatures on this planet and in what ways different. He will want to know in what ways human beings are all alike and in what ways different, group by group and individual by individual.

Of course, you may very well decide to leave the explanations to somebody else. But if you decide to stay and try, you will first have to tell him what it means to be human. And to do this, perhaps it will be just as well to start with human beginnings. . . .

PART ONE
KIN AND KIND

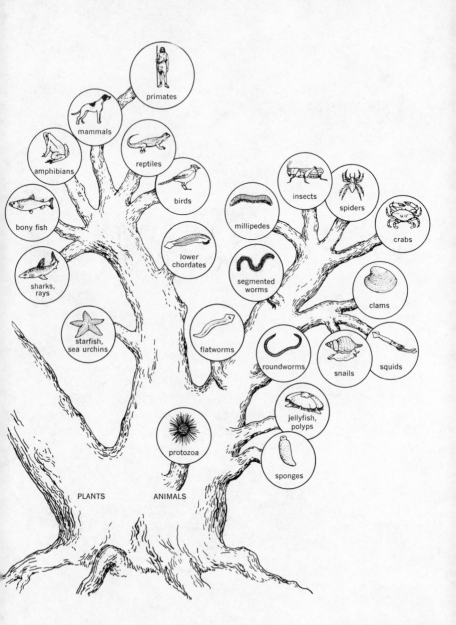

1

CLIMBING OUR FAMILY TREE
The Importance of Being Related

To be human is to be something unique in the world, true. Still, for all that, we are only the latest blossoms on the tree of life. And we should never have produced a bud without all the twigs and branches and stately limbs that lifted us up. Nothing of our vaunted human culture, our consciousness, or our symbols could have been achieved without the hands and eyes of the primates, the warm blood and maternal instinct of the mammals, and the wonderful chordate backbone tipped at one end with sensory swellings which—enormously enlarged, overgrown, and expanded—would one day become the human brain.

The debt does not end there. Our heritage extends all the way down the trunk of the tree of life, into the world of inorganic matter. For it is from this world that all substance is drawn and all shadow, all shape, all form. From the unimaginably small to the unimaginably vast, it is the interplay of matter and energy that binds the whole of being in one mighty web. So tightly woven are the strands, so dependent each part on each, so interlocking the segments and levels of existence, that the destruction of any part can unalterably affect the whole. Indeed, the British astronomer Fred Hoyle believes that were even a piece of the universe to be removed—as by some cosmic hand dipping chestnuts from a bowl—our own solar system would behave quite differently. "No man is an island, entire of itself," said the poet John Donne. Why then, it would seem that no planet is an island, either, nor a planetary system, nor any portion of the great universe.

Whatever our ties with that universe eventually prove to be, whatever the human position in the vast scheme of things, we know at least this: the building blocks in the heart of a star are also to be found in our own bodies—or in any stone. For hydrogen, the simplest and lightest of all atoms, turns up (shorn of its electron) as an indispensable nuclear particle in every other atom.

At the elementary atomic level—beyond eyesight and almost beyond understanding—there is little meaning to the words *life* and *nonlife*. There all is motion, some rapid, some slow, in patterns which curiously ape the swinging spheres. Electrons, many or few, orbit their enormously larger nuclei much as planets of our solar system orbit their star. These minute systems merge with others of like or differing order to form "galaxies" which begin to be tangible to our senses. All this in a stone which seems to lie so cold and still in a warm human hand. And yet from the invisible sub-atomic dimension of some stones are emitted high-energy rays or particles which, all unseen and unsus-pected, can invade realms of being far above the micro-cosm and wreak unalterable destruction in a living cell. In any cell—be it small as an amoeba or large as an ostrich egg's yolk, be it plant or animal.

It is with the cell that life as we know it begins. In a larger frame by far, quite beyond the dervish dance of the charged particles, each visible fragment of stone appears as stilled, inert matter. Yet, in the cell, many of the stone's atomic constituents have mysteriously assembled into a form which moves and reacts to stimuli, adjusts, feeds, and dies. Each cell is geared to self-preservation, and each carries within its nucleus rodlike chromosomes—the blueprints for self-duplica-tion. As each cell divides to multiply, so the chromo-somes divide equally, forming anew to hold the pattern of form and function intact.

Each cell contains within its miniscule self factories for the processing of food into energy. Some cells came early to capture the energy of the sun itself for the pro-duction of food from water and carbon dioxide and were thus the first green plants. Soon began that inti-mate relationship between plant and animal life which

A CELL DIVIDES TO
FORM TWO NEW CELLS
THAT ARE IDENTICAL

continued through all the many transformations each
was in time to undergo. It continues still.

Life evolved in a watery environment—shallow seas
in which all wants were provided. Nutrients and gases,
liquid borne, seeped through semi-permeable boundaries into cellular plasma. Wastes seeped out the same
way into the surrounding sea. Oxygen, given off by
sunlit plant cells as waste, diffused to the later-appear-
ing animal cells for which it fired the engines of life.
The animal cells' carbon-dioxide exhaust in turn helped
to support the plant cells. Both gases, accumulating as
the cells multiplied, eventually escaped the incubating
sea into the earth's atmosphere.

We are still creatures of the sea which gave us birth.
And the human body's countless cells—organized in
colonies, in organs specialized to their separate and
interlocking tasks—still operate in a perpetual bath.
Through it nutrients are diffused and gases exchanged
in the selfsame manner of the primordial cell borne on
a warm sea tide. Our body's fluid, if not quite of the
same constitution as that sea, still recalls in its saltiness
the ancient home. We are, in fact, mostly water—shake
us and we slosh; drop us and we splatter—and our
fancy suits of skin serve less to keep rain out than to
keep moisture in.

The potential for human life (and for all life) lies in
a cell, in the female reproductive egg, which oddly pos-
sesses only half its complement of chromosomes. When
it is joined by a male reproductive cell, similarly short

on chromosomes, the two halves fuse to form one whole cell which—dividing, then, to multiply in the way of all cells—will one day become a human being. The finished product will be in many ways wholly unique, for the mingling of parent cells and their inherited traits permits endless variation on a theme. It is this capacity for variation which has, over the long years, shaped the world of living things and which shapes us still.

The fertilized reproductive cell in its progress toward the human form retraces many of the intricate pathways life has taken in the past. Each human being is fated to climb anew his family tree on the way to his final destination. From the cell to a small colony of undifferentiated cells he goes; to a three-layered community, each layer with its special function and organ potential. Rather like a little sponge he is very briefly, and then a blind and coiling thing with the rough beginnings of a gut and a primitive streak along the line of which nerve ends will eventually form and ravel in a cord.

After a month of growth the human embryo has decidedly arrived at the vertebrate stage, but just *which* vertebrate is hard to tell offhand. This anonymous living thing could as easily be the embryo of a salamander or a chick or a rat as of a man. Like them all, the human embryo is provided with a nutrient-filled yolk sac. Like them all, he bravely sprouts a tail. His developing heart is at first two-chambered like the fish's

SOME VERTEBRATE EMBRYOS

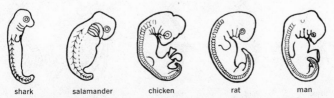

shark   salamander   chicken   rat   man

heart. Fishlike, he comes equipped with gill pouches which, never slitting, eventually form the chamber of his middle ear, his tonsils, and various glands. A fretwork of gill bars gives him part of his jaws, his middle-ear bones, some cartilage in his throat, and the platform for his tongue, even as they provided his vertebrate ancestors long ago. If you have ever seen a tadpole just emerging from its jelly casing, you have seen the prototype of the embryonic vertebrate form. Like one, like all.

It is not to be supposed that in his life before birth a beginning human being resembles the final adult forms of his vertebrate kin any more than they resemble each other. He resembles their embryos. Only in the embryo's watery egg-world do likenesses emerge and family patterns show plain. Only here does he briefly revisit the way stations of his physical heritage. And here occur those minute changes in the basic body plan which, at long, long last, guarantee a new sort of being and still another branch on the family tree.

Still and all, man's relationships as an adult creature with the mature forms of other vertebrates can be traced with a little probing and imagination. Long before Charles Darwin had guessed a way of transformation in living forms, animals had been classified as to their degree of resemblance with other animals. Today we can read those similarities and differences in the light of the basic bony plan which was the major

SOME VERTEBRATE ARMS

lizard   bird   bat   whale   man

contribution of the first vertebrate creature to our branch of the family tree. A whale's fluke, for instance, a bat's wing, a reptile's forelimb, a man's hand and arm: though performing different functions, they contain the same bones in the same numbers. (Not, however, in the same shapes or sizes.) And the skeletal numbers game can be played with the bones of any vertebrate creature.

In the soft interior parts, similar organs, similar glands, and similar nervous systems work in much the same ways. Vertebrates of the sea need less in the way of complicated equipment than creatures of the land and have less accordingly. Air-breathers need and have more up-to-date plumbing, ventilating, and heating equipment. Mammals are most modern of all. Still, a stomach is a stomach, a kidney is a kidney, and all may be compared. Even our mammalian lung, the indispensable organ for land life, is recognizable in the swim bladder of a modern fish. The very fluids and secretions of the body tell, in their chemical constitution, of close or distant kinship with other vertebrate forms.

The human body is a walking museum filled with relics of its still living past. The last vestige of a tail can be seen in the curled-under tip of our spine, the coccyx. Muscles that once made it lift or wag have bent to the burden of our internal organs which, in view of man's upright posture need all the support they can get.

Everyone is familiar with the appendix, that dead-

SKELETONS OF
MAN AND APE

end little "worm" off the large intestine which sends so many sufferers to the hospital. Useless now, it may once have served a digestive function when the diet of our ancestors was rather different from our present one.

And then there is the "third eye," a little red body between the hemispheres of our brain, without a window to the world. When early vertebrate life occupied the sandy bottoms of shallow waters, food below and enemies above, the pineal eye must have served an important function. It watched and warned. Perhaps it triggered a protective color transformation in time of danger. Its opening in the skulls of mobile, modern fishes has long since closed over. But lampreys and some lizards still retain a tiny window for the "third eye" which, though buried under a layer of skin, can at least sense changes in darkness and light. No one quite knows how the pineal body functions for us if it functions at all. Perhaps it secretes some glandular substance, or perhaps it is as useless as the appendix without being so troublesome.

Gooseflesh still appears on our skin in winter in a vain effort to fluff up our nonexistent fur and keep us warm. Our ears sometimes grow with unhuman points, and sometimes we can wiggle them with muscles which once could tip them toward the source of sound and sharpen hearing. Our sensitive human facial expressions are produced by muscles which long ago served to aerate a fish's gills.

Even in the proudest of our physical possessions the

record of the past is not erased. Hidden under the gray, cauliflower-like cerebrum—which is what comes first to mind at the mention of "brain"—lies the old brain, stem, core, and cerebellum. Little more than an enlargement of the neural tube inside the spine, this old brain directs muscular activity, receives impressions from ear and eye, helps regulate (all without conscious effort) the functioning of the vital organs, and stores who knows what half-forgotten instincts, what half-remembered fears. From the gray frontal swellings of the core (wherein the sense of smell had its home) began that monstrous cerebral overgrowth which sets us apart from our vertebrate kin.

As the sense of smell lost importance, the cerebrum specialized for other activities. Its outer layer (the cortex) wrinkled and doubled on itself, constantly infolding as the surface span increased. Here came to reside memory and imagination, will and choice, and all the sorted, correlated welter of sensory perceptions which bind past to future and reason to desire. We still do not know exactly how this wrinkled mass works. Some of its areas have clear associations with speech and hearing and movement. Others, seemingly, are "blank spots." Perhaps these serve as file cabinets in which are stored packets of impressions and recordings of experiences lived and forgotten.

However it works, the cerebrum cannot work alone. All its directions must detour through the old brain to get action. Altogether, it is an elaboration of form and

SOME VERTEBRATE BRAINS

shark

lizard

rabbit

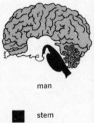

man

■ stem
□ core
▨ cerebellum
▨ cerebrum

substance vastly beyond the bare needs of animal existence. Yet because of that elaboration, I can write about
the brain, and you can read what I have written. And
we are joined in a cultural elaboration which is itself
far beyond man's basic needs. This is the whole of
being human.

In the next chapters we will shinny backward down
the family tree, pausing here and there to visit our relatives and pass the time of day.

ORANGUTAN

2

MAN AMONG THE PRIMATES
A View from the Upper Branches

In climbing our part of the family tree, we and our primate relatives have stayed pretty close to the trunk. Among the primates there are no radical specialties as in other mammals—the giraffe's long neck, for instance, or the whale's body, streamlined for the sea. It is true, of course, that animals which do become closely geared to their natural environment—its temperatures, foods, dangers, and protection—are able to make the best of life. Often they manage to push aside their more conservative competitors. But if, in specializing, such animals get too far out on an evolutionary limb, too narrowly suited to the surroundings, they may find themselves out of luck when those surroundings change —and out of life as well. Generalized animals may not always offer keen competition, but they are better able to adapt to change and to hang on longer and to climb the family tree.

Primates, by and large, stayed generalized because they literally (as well as figuratively) kept to the tree. Our very first mammal ancestors skittered nervously in and out of trees. And evolving primates just never left home—until much later in the game, that is.

Tree living offers a good bit of protection, but it has drawbacks, too. A creature can be just as dead of a fall from thirty feet up as from a crunching in some predator's mouth. To get along comfortably in the trees a creature needs agility, awareness, and quick responses; he must do lots of things well and nothing too much. Tree living has consistently favored such jacks-of-all-trades and consigned the rest to early extinction. So it is no wonder that the continuing evolutionary trend among primates has always been toward steady improvement on an already efficient plan.

Good grasping hands are important for tree dwellers, and primates come so equipped. Most have opposable thumbs (and opposable big toes too). Between thumb and fingers, even the tiniest object can be turned, pinched, manipulated ever so precisely, ever so delicately. With his own primate hands, man came at last to make weapons and plowshares, music and art.

man

With the development of the grasping hand, conventional claws seem very quickly to have gone out of style. They were replaced in most primates by nails

SOME PRIMATE HANDS

tree shrew   tarsier   baboon   orangutan   gorilla

which protected the finger ends but kept neatly out of the way. Grasping hands apparently made tails expendable too, at least among the Old World monkeys, who scarcely know what to do with their rear appendages. The higher primates have lost their tails altogether (though we have more of a vestige than the apes). With monkeys of the New World—cut off from their relatives very early in primate evolution—it is quite a different story. They have kept their tails and use them prehensilely, as combination safety belts, tentacles, and hanging hooks. But their hands are, correspondingly, less well developed.

BRACHIATING
APE

The ball-and-socket shoulder joint—so useful to baseball pitchers—is another by-product of tree living. In later evolutionary days, the apes carried this flexibility to extremes, swinging through the trees, hand over hand—a form of locomotion known as brachiating. Fortune favored individuals best adapted to such athletics—those with enormously lengthened arms and shortened legs and thumbs. Our own direct ancestors apparently came down from the trees and left off brachiating before it got to be a bad habit. Human gymnasts can still brachiate nearly as well as a chimpanzee. But, of course, no ape can walk upright for very long at a time. That is our own particular specialty.

SOME PRIMATE FEET

chimpanzee   forest gorilla   mountain gorilla   man

Still and all, we do owe our upright posture ultimately to tree living. The need to hang from branches and shinny up and down boles seems to have favored individuals with bodies increasingly inclined to the vertical. The pelvis of apes, for example, tucks under a good bit to support the internal organs, though not, of course, with so pronounced a "floor" as our own pelvic underpinning provides. The feature of next importance in maintaining an upright stance is the foot, perhaps the most specialized of all our primate physical equipment. Even this is approached in shape by the foot of the mountain gorilla, whose girth eventually forced him down from the trees.

SHRINKING THE SNOUT

In response to tree living and its rigors, the sense of smell wanes as the importance of good eyesight waxes. Primates sniff less and look more. They examine objects with their flexible fingers, holding them up to their eyes. A long muzzle with which to nose unfamiliar things about becomes unnecessary. And so with very early primates we can see the beginnings of a face. (An exception to this trend is the baboon, whose later adaptation to life on the ground probably contributed to his doglike muzzle and four-footed gait.)

The decreasing muzzle in primates may also be a case of architectural revision to accommodate the growing brain. For grow it did. The American anthropologist W. W. Howells says that both apes and men have more brain than ever they use in daily life and cites the unusual capacities of apes in captivity to prove the

early fish

stem reptile

mammal-like reptile

early mammal

fossil lemur

fossil monkey

man

point. Whatever the degree of use, it seems certain that part of the brain's growth (more specifically, the growth of the cerebral cortex) was due to the importance of good eyesight in tree living. The visual centers at the back of the cerebrum are much larger in monkeys than in other animals, and largest of all in man. A large visual center means, certainly, a richer variety of impressions received, recorded, correlated, and stored. Everyone knows how inquisitive monkeys are. This curiosity (of such great consequence for human kind) could be connected with the heightened visual input to the primate brain through ever better primate eyes.

With the shrinking of the snout, the nasal barrier between the eyes was removed, allowing the fields of vision to overlap. Instead of two pictures with a space in between, primates, far back in their evolution, began to see one picture in depth and possibly in color. This is stereoscopic vision, and how useful it must have been in jumping from one branch to the next not to see a gap where a handhold ought to be.

It must not be thought, however, that tree living automatically calls forth the same set of physical adaptations every time, in every animal, in the same serial order. Opossums and squirrels did not come to resemble primates simply because they happened to share the same home address. Each came to terms with nature in its own particular way.

It is true that species do change in time because special environments favor individuals adjusted physically in such a way as to get along better in them. But the environment itself does not make the adjustments happen. The environment can only work with what it gets, and what it gets is determined elsewhere. Changes—mutations—appear before an ever so slightly different creature's birth. They occur, in fact, even before he is properly begun. It is in the reproductive cells of his parents-to-be, in their chromosomes, that the genes—those blueprints of heredity—are altered to produce a "new" creature.

Some scientists think that chromosomes may be broken, kinked, or looped in odd ways as a result of background radiation—cosmic rays, perhaps, or natural radioactivity from the soil—entering the reproductive cells. Whatever the cause, gene changes do happen, and changed individuals are born.

If their differentness (usually so slight as to be scarcely noticeable) proves useful, they thrive better than their kindred, live longer, and have more offspring, some of which will also exhibit the new and useful trait. If the trait does not give any particular advantage it may persist—underground, you might say—perhaps to come in handy at some future time. It may simply be diluted in the general gene pool—that is, the collection of possible traits shared by all the members of a species.

If the new trait is harmful, however, the changed animal will die early, possibly before he can pass it on to unfortunate offspring. Sometimes animals at opposite ends of a range of possible appearances and characteristics mate, producing offspring in which the extremes are so mingled as to result in individuals rather different from either parent—pioneers of a new type altogether.

With all these "ifs" in mind, you can see why not all primate trends were carried through in all primates. Slow climbers have stopped at all stages of development and, protected from competition in out-of-the-way places, survive today. We are, in fact, particularly lucky in having living examples of our checkered primate past. Not all the levels are represented, of course; there are plenty of gaps. Enough of the picture is filled in, however, to give us some notion of our beginnings.

Tupaia, the tree shrew, probably stands closer than any other living primate to the tiny, insect-eating mammal who was ancestor to us all. It belongs to the first subdivision of the primate order: the prosimians—before monkeys. Some very early prosimians apparently went out on an evolutionary limb in trying to compete with the fast-growing rodent tribe. Their fossil skulls and teeth, in fact, show a remarkable resemblance to those of some living squirrels. The innovation did not work, however, and all of these types very quickly fell off the family tree.

Although ancient tree shrews may have been widely distributed, living specimens are confined to Southeast Asia and the Philippines. The tree shrew much pre-

TREE SHREW

fers insects to any other diet. But in spite of its rodent-like appearance and sharp claws, it has fair grasping hands and detectably better vision and poorer smell than other insect-eating mammals, such as ground shrews or hedgehogs, once thought to be the tree shrew's close relatives. The tree shrew also has a bigger brain, and that—along with its hands and eyes—has given it a primate rather than an insectivore classification.

Still among the prosimians but further up the branch are the lemurs, all of which are today to be found only on Madagascar and nearby islands, and the more cosmopolitan lorises. Fossil species date back nearly to the beginning of the Age of Mammals, roughly 60 million years ago. Their living representatives are still essentially primitive when compared to other, more progressive primates. Some species produce babies in litters, and the mothers have extra equipment for nursing a crowd. The concentration on quality rather than quantity in offspring apparently came later on and higher up the evolutionary scale, possibly as a continuing adaptation to tree living. Some lemur types make devoted parents in spite of the overwork involved.

RING-TAILED
LEMUR

Between the prosimians and the higher primates is the tarsier with its padded digits, appealing face, and enormous nighttime eyes. The tarsier has lost altogether the moist muzzle of the lower primates and acquired a real upper lip. It is especially adapted for jumping with the enormously elongated foot bone

TARSIER

(*tarsus*) which gives it a name. It relishes insects but often stalks lizards, about the biggest prey it can comfortably manage. Tarsier couples are said to stick together inseparably and produce only one baby at a time.

The jump up from the prosimian level is a big one, for the rest of the limb is labelled *Anthropoidea*—the manlike ones. It includes all the monkeys and the apes and ourselves.

First we come to the South American monkeys—the Platyrrhini, or broad noses. In their evolution from a

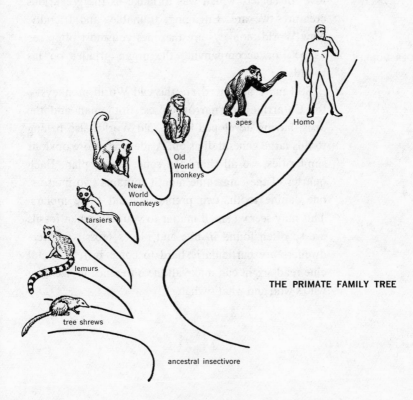

apes Homo

Old World monkeys

New World monkeys

tarsiers

lemurs

THE PRIMATE FAMILY TREE

tree shrews

ancestral insectivore

NEW WORLD
SPIDER MONKEY

primitive prosimian ancestry, they were entirely separated from their cousins in the Old World. Interest-
ingly enough, they developed along much the same lines
anyhow. The Panama land bridge between the northern
and southern continents submerged at the end of the
dinosaur era and did not reappear until the last ice age
set in, a million or so years ago. By that time, the prosimians which had been common in North America all
through the early years of the Age of Mammals had,
for some reason, vanished utterly.

New World monkeys are noisy and inoffensive. They
congregate in chattering clusters, typifying the primate
love for society which was to make us the gregarious
creatures we are. Engaging, trainable, and friendly,
New World monkeys are the ones you most often see
as pets or accompanying the organ grinder on his
rounds.

Still more advanced are the Old World monkeys—
the Catarrhini, or narrow noses. Both man and the
apes, having developed in the Old World, also belong
to this large general division. Aside from more obvious
similarities, we all share the same dental plan. Each
quarter of the catarrhine mouth contains two incisors,
one canine tooth, two premolars, and three molars.
This may seem a small matter to you, but when fossils
are so often found in bits and pieces (fossils of tree-
dwellers are particularly hard to come by), a dental
clue read aright can make all the difference in deciding
who's who and what's what.

Among Old World monkeys are the familiar rhesus, our test pilot in space and hero of many a laboratory experiment; Barbary apes of Gibraltar, who really are not apes at all; and baboons. Biggest and most formidable of all monkeys, the ground-dwelling, tribal baboons have certainly struck the human fancy. Folklore has praised them as "good soldiers," exaggerated their abilities, and condemned their manners. They have even been called "outright fascists." Some anthropologists have wondered whether their behavior as ground primates could tell us anything about early man, who was himself earthbound. Because baboon behavior has always seemed incredibly bumptious, aggressive, and domineering, it tended to color for a time the thinking about early man. All forgotten was the fact that most baboon studies had been made in zoos. Few human beings, I venture to say, would behave very normally when locked up in jail. And neither do baboons in zoos. Recent observations of these primates on their home grounds tell us that the truth lies somewhere between folklore and zoo behavior. It is true that baboons travel in large "troops" carefully guarded by the strong adult males. It is true that these troops tend to be rather more disciplined than the social groupings of apes and other monkeys, less easygoing, more self-contained. But baboons do not seem to be unnecessarily aggressive—either among themselves or with other primates. Certainly their adaptation to the ground has been successful. Even the advance of civilization in

BABOON

Africa has not noticeably cramped the baboon's style.

The apes and man are lumped together in a category labeled *Hominoidea,* which roughly means the same thing as *Anthropoidea* except that the root of one is Latin and the other Greek. The new term implies still more manlike beings, however, so we are climbing again.

Rather later than monkeys on the time scale—on the order of 30 million years ago—the first hominoids appeared. Fossil evidences have been scanty as yet, but the picture they suggest is that of a small, tailless, rather generalized creature, reminiscent in some ways of monkeys, in others of the great apes, and in still others of man. And there is something different about the teeth of hominoids—especially as we move upward in time with them. If you run a finger (or your tongue) over your own molar teeth, you will feel little points, or hills, called "cusps." Now, the cusps of monkey teeth come four to the molar. But the pattern for the hominoids is five to the tooth, arranged roughly along the spaces of a *Y*. This is called the Y-5, or *Dryopithecus,* pattern after the fossil ape in whose jaw teeth it was first noted.

Smallest of the living hominoids are the gibbons and siamangs, whose aerial acrobatics are something to behold. They are prodigious singers, too, with inflatable air sacs in their necks to enhance tone and volume. In any zoo you can hear the calls and cries of the gibbons above the combined din of all the other animals. In

GIBBON

MONKEY TOOTH   HOMINOID TOOTH

their Southeast Asian forests, gibbons much prefer the company of spouse and offspring to that of the group, a pattern rather foreign to the usual primate sociability. Even gibbon offspring are rudely pushed out of the family at adolescence.

The living great apes include the orangutans, the chimpanzees, and the gorillas. Orangs, however, look like nothing so much as a caricature of the lot. Their color scheme is garish—shaggy orange hair over bright chocolate skin. Their faces—especially those of the large, powerful males—are framed, moonlike, in a great fleshy hoop. In the middle, all but buried, are a pair of tiny eyes, a miniature nose, and a slit of a mouth. Like gibbons, orangs are Asiatic, brachiating, and equipped with inflatable air sacs. Although intelligent, they are even less social than the gibbons and really prefer to live alone.

The great apes have been called man's poor relations. And this is especially true of the African chimpanzee and gorilla. They share our curiosity, something of our cleverness, our diseases, and our parasites. Like the baboons, they have most often been studied in captivity. There they usually prove to be amiable subjects, using their minds with astounding capability. But studies in confinement have not told all. Observers who have learned to live with gorillas and chimpanzees almost as adopted members of the group, traveling with them over home territory by day, sleeping under their tree-beds by night, report abilities and behavior we

GORILLA

have never before suspected. Both gorillas and chimpanzees are gentler and kinder with one another than
zoo studies indicate. Both show concern for their sick
and old, and learn their ways of behaving from moth-
erly instruction (even as we do). Chimpanzees especially have a wide range of sound signals and often
communicate with gestures very like our own. Both
gorilla and chimpanzee males indulge in ritual display
—a kind of dance pantomime to let off steam or to
brag or simply to follow a tradition. We don't know.

Observers in zoo and forest say the ponderous gorilla
tends to be withdrawn and shy, though there are individual differences in temperament. In the forest, gorillas, though not exactly unemotional, tend to be a good
deal more dignified and restrained than the boisterous
chimpanzee.

The chimpanzee is our closest poor relation, the
cousin who shares the same blood substances, the same
facial expressions, and the same high spirits. Chimpanzees show great individuality in personality and ability.
Even in the matter of social groupings almost anything
goes. Chimpanzee bands in Africa have been observed
to divide and reunite casually as various fruits ripen.
Friends toddle off together; parties of bachelors go
about stag; mothers with babies congregate as fancy
dictates. Chimps are easygoing among themselves and
will not fight even when faced with a romantic triangle.
In East Africa, chimpanzees have been seen, not only
to use twigs as tools, but to modify them as well.

Like us, all the higher primates concentrate on fewer babies and longer periods of maternal care. Baby apes are more helpless at birth, and helpless for a longer time, than monkey babies. Human babies are most helpless of all. Throughout the first three years of life, the chimpanzee child is in every way (except in the matter of speech) the peer and often the superior of his human counterpart. Then he reaches his limit. The human child—his skull bones elastic and growing still to accommodate his expanding brain—goes on to read and write and plan and do, leaving his cousin, his closest poor relation, far, far behind.

CHIMPANZEE WITH A STICK

3

MAN AMONG THE MAMMALS
Adding Mother

Mice and men, moles and bats, dogs and cats—all are brothers under their coats of hair (thick or thin as the case may be). We all share a common ancestor, an insect-eating mammal perhaps quite like the tree shrew, mentioned earlier as the first of the primates. He was a very small, very insignificant ancestor. He had to be unobtrusive, for he lived during the Mesozoic Era—the Age of Middle Life—when dinosaurs ruled the earth, and his life depended on the ability to make himself scarce. It wasn't nearly so much a problem of being made a snack as of being stepped on during some monster's ponderous march to the swamp.

For all his tiny size and humble station, this little insectivore outlived and outlasted the reptile kings. He may even have contributed to their extinction by slyly eating their eggs—though, of course, that would not begin to explain their disappearance altogether. There were geologic changes at the end of the Mesozoic. It was at this time that the Rocky Mountains were being uplifted in North America, the Andes in South America, and the Alps in Europe. Familiar swamplands were drained dry and deserts appeared where none had been before. Doubtless there were changes too in the climate and in the life patterns of many creatures. Perhaps the accustomed fodder for the plant-eating dinosaurs disappeared, leaving them to die of starvation. Their predators, the mighty meat eaters, would surely have followed them into extinction. Whatever the changes were—and no one knows exactly—they were widespread. For it was not only the great reptiles of the land that vanished but those of the sea and air as well. There were left only lizards, snakes, turtles, and crocodiles to represent the reptiles on earth. But early mammals survived the revolution handily. They were equipped for change, and because of them, so are we.

They had, first of all, warm blood (as do we). Reptiles are "cold-blooded," a misleading sort of description, really, because they are neither nasty-tempered by nature nor is their blood really "cold." Their temperature is simply determined by the temperature outside their bodies. In frosty weather, reptiles are sluggish or inert. When the mercury soars, so do their internal temperatures. Mammals, on the other hand, come provided with thermostatically controlled furnaces which maintain a steady internal temperature regardless of the weather. (Of course there *are* extremes beyond which even this sophisticated machinery will not operate.) Some mammals are able to lower the thermostat, going into hibernation during cold weather. Birds, who share with us the gift of warm blood, fly south to avoid the cold.

As insulation for their heating units, early mammals had protective coats of hair which, in cold weather, automatically fluffed up, creating an added layer of insulating air between fur and skin. Most members of the family have kept this hair. Only the aquatic mammals (whales, hippos, some seals) and elephants, rhinos, and ourselves have turned very nearly bald all over. Some scholars think this has resulted from forays into new environments: the sea for whales, culture for man. But this does not explain the baldness of elephants and rhinos, stay-putters who were sporting fur coats only yesterday during the Ice Age.

Hair and fur are as useful in the blazing sunshine as in the freezing shade. They protect and insulate. Mammals, nevertheless, go still one step further in the matter of temperature regulation. They possess evaporative coolers, just as they must have in their beginnings. In hot weather, sweat pours from glands which may be stationed all over the body, as in man, or just here and there. As moisture evaporates, the skin is cooled and so is the blood beneath the skin and, with circulation, so is the rest of the body.

Early mammals probably lived life at a higher pitch and a faster pace than reptiles. They were active and inventive, capable of quick reactions and quick bursts of energy in time of danger. Their bodies were geared to speed and efficiency. Better teeth did a thorough processing job on food (no more wholesale gulping as was the reptile way) so that nourishment could be quickly converted into energy. A four-chambered heart divided blood freshly supplied with oxygen from used blood carrying carbon dioxide lungward. Early mammals therefore got more energy from each breath than did the reptiles. And breaths themselves were bigger, thanks to better respiratory muscles—a diaphragm underneath the lungs, for instance. Altogether, the mammal body was a decided refinement on the reptilian plan.

There was something different about mammal brains, too. Perhaps not so startlingly different in the beginning, but certainly as time went on. They were larger, for one thing, and the covering of the cerebral hemispheres, the cortex (almost nonexistent in reptilian forms), was beginning to expand over the smelling portions of the older brain. This new growth reinforced life based more on learning, less on instinct, so that each creature could be—in however small a measure— different from his peers, different from those who had come before and who would come after. Learning and the capacity for learning goes along with one other fact of mammalian life: Mother.

MOTHER SHREW WITH A
CARAVAN OF OFFSPRING

Mammal babies are born alive. They do not hatch from a shell, unnoticed and untended. For weeks and months they develop in leisurely fashion, protected from chance and from the elements by a mother's body. Like reptiles, they begin embryonic life supplied with a yolk sac, but when its nutriments are exhausted, they need not, like reptile babies, be thrust rudely into the world. In most mammals nourishment from the mother's bloodstream, diffusing across a special membrane (the placenta), enters the embryo's bloodstream to give continued life. Wastes are carried off in the same way. Altogether, the mammal embryo is the perfect parasite.

There were many evolutionary attempts to achieve this state of affairs. Some fish and reptiles retain their eggs internally until they are ready to hatch. Marine reptiles of the Age of Dinosaurs, the ichthyosaurs, gave birth to newly hatched young in much the same way as mammalian dolphins today: tail first, thus keeping the infant from drowning during labor. But only placental mammals have "solved" the problem of true internal nourishment. Still living are two types of primitive mammals whose ways of giving birth may illustrate the evolutionary steps in between. Monotremes (so called because of their single external opening which serves both excretory and reproductive functions) lay eggs. And marsupials, such as the kangaroo and bandicoot, bring forth unformed little fetuses which must complete their development in the mother's

OPOSSUM MOTHER
WITH HER YOUNG

external pouch (or *marsupium*). Both monotremes and marsupials have survived only in Australia or on nearby islands, protected there from the competition of later, hardier, more efficient placental mammals. The lone exception is the marsupial opossum which, against all odds, has continued to thrive and increase in the Western Hemisphere.

Propelled by instinct, reptile babies emerge from the egg fully able to fend for themselves. They have to be; nobody else is going to do the job. This is fine for survival, but with every action so neatly precomputed, very little leeway is left for learning. Baby mammals, on the other hand, arrive in a fairly helpless condition, utterly dependent on their mothers. They must be protected and they must be fed a special food. This food—milk—is supplied by the mother's mammary glands (from which mammals get their name).

During their infancy, little mammals (all pliable as they are and considerably less marked by instinct than their reptile counterparts) learn from their mother. She teaches them to protect themselves, to hunt if they are meat eaters, to venture, and to travel. Most of all they learn from her how to be good parents themselves against the day when their own babies will arrive. From this uniquely mammal combination of mother and child (determined though it was in part by glandular processes) there began a new trend. It was to lead in time to more complex social relationships among primates—and finally to human altruism and human love.

Hair and temperature, intelligence and mammary glands are all very helpful in claiming kin with living mammals. But we can not use these traits in tracking ancestry, where all we have to go by are bones. Fortunately, these provide a great many clues. The fossil skeletons of early reptiles tend to be heavy, clumsy, with limbs so splayed and spread it must have taken a real effort just to heave the living body up off the ground. Many of today's reptiles still have limbs set in the old pattern. Bones of land mammals, today and yesterday, however, are lighter, fewer in number, better composed. The limbs tuck neatly under the body for better support and leverage. Far from being pushed against the earth, chained by the weight of gravity, mammals, with all their quickness and lightness, often seem ready to leave it. Many, in fact, do all their walking on their tiptoes—some even on their toenails.

A REPTILE SKULL

Mammal skulls are more ample than those of reptiles, scaled to accommodate bigger brains. Their middle ears contain three little bones for sound conduction instead of the reptilian single one, the additions having been formed from excess lower jaw parts. The mammal skull has an extra palate which permits the owner to breathe while chewing food. The skeletal nose has only one external opening instead of the reptile's two. And there is a big difference in teeth. Those of reptiles are simply pointed pegs, all alike and forever growing, forever replaceable. The teeth of even the earlier mammals show variety. Some grind, some gnash, some pierce.

A MAMMAL SKULL

Later mammals (primates excepted) developed many dental specialties—the elephant's tusks, the rodent's chisels. But we, one and all, get only two complete sets in a lifetime, and when they are gone, no more teeth unless we can manage artificial ones.

All these skeletal characteristics can be found a long way back in time. Remains of the first true mammals date to the middle of dinosaur times, 180 million years or so ago. *Their* ancestors are even older. There is good reason to believe that these ancestral creatures—called collectively "mammal-like reptiles" because that is clearly what they were—may have been the very first branch off the reptilian stem. And this occurred close to 280 million years ago, long before the more spectacular dinosaurs appeared.

The first mammal-like reptiles lived toward the end of the Paleozoic Era, the Age of Old Life. It was a time of geologic upheavals somewhat like those that marked the end of the dinosaur age. There were glaciers over part of the earth then, and change and cold. Some scientists think the early appearance of mammal-like characteristics shows adaptation to this

FINNED-BACK PELYCOSAUR

new sort of environment, much like the response of later mammals to the changes in *their* world. During this time, the pelycosaurs (which were the dominant life form) began to show signs of tooth variation and a decided improvement in bony structure. Some sported great bony sails on their backs. The purpose of these strange contraptions nobody knows. Perhaps they functioned as heat conductors, bringing the sun's warmth more quickly to the night-sluggish reptilian body. Meat eaters with sails, like the early bird after the worm, would be able to get breakfast before their still-torpid companions knew what had happened to them.

More advanced mammal-like reptiles (the therapsids), which lived somewhat later, at the beginning of the Mesozoic Era, were quicker, lighter, and more streamlined than the pelycosaurs. Even the gawky ones had their legs tucked well under their bodies and displayed a diversity of teeth. One of them must have looked for all the world like a cross between a lizard and a dog and is called, aptly enough, *Cynognathus* ("dog jaw"). Whether or not the therapsids had begun to mother their young and give them milk we do not know. Perhaps that living fossil the duck-billed platypus may provide a clue. So different is it (and its cousin monotreme, the spiny anteater) from the rest of living mammals, with so many reptilian characteristics that the American paleontologist G. G. Simpson has called it a modified therapsid, alive beyond its

A THERAPSID

time. Certainly the platypus antedates the other mammals. The female lays leathery-skinned eggs which she warms and broods over. When they hatch, she feeds the babies milk which drips like sweat from unlocalized chest pores. Perhaps the family life of mammal-like reptiles followed such a plan.

Many therapsids were meat eaters and looked it. Like most hunters, they ran to speed and brains. When the great meat-eating dinosaurs came along to dominate the stage, perhaps 225 million years ago, the mammal-like reptiles took their leave, crowded out by competition. But they left descendants behind—inoffensive little creatures, already in four varieties—along with the persistent monotremes. From one of the four, *Pantothere* ("all animal"), would come the future marsupial and placental mammals of the world.

During the Cenozoic Era, the Age of Recent Life, early mammals began to branch out, diversifying, changing to fit the vacated living-rooms of the earth. Some stayed teaspoon-small. Some grew to be house-sized. Bats took to the air where frightful pterosaurs had once flown. Whales and, later, seals and manatees

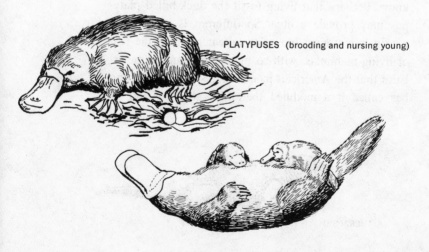

PLATYPUSES (brooding and nursing young)

MAMMAL BEGINNINGS

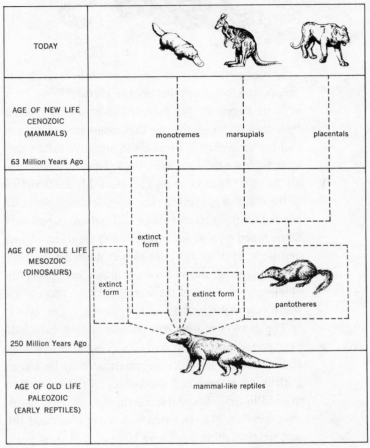

TODAY	
AGE OF NEW LIFE CENOZOIC (MAMMALS) 63 Million Years Ago	monotremes marsupials placentals
AGE OF MIDDLE LIFE MESOZOIC (DINOSAURS) 250 Million Years Ago	extinct form extinct form extinct form pantotheres
AGE OF OLD LIFE PALEOZOIC (EARLY REPTILES)	mammal-like reptiles

went back to the sea where reptilian ichthyosaurs, plesiosaurs, and mosasaurs had once reigned.

Some mammals very soon fell to eating their neighbors, thus taking on the role that carnivorous dinosaurs
had formerly played. From these primitive meat eaters
were to come the later cats, dogs, bears, weasels, and
all the other hunters, except for man. Mammal victims
of the carnivores evolved their own defenses. Some depended on fleetness of foot or took refuge in numbers.
Some relied on size and strength and stoutness of tusk
and horn, even as *Triceratops* had done before them.
And filling out the in-between areas, occupying the
chinks and crannies of the world, were the rodents, the
burrowing moles, and the early primates.

The dawn of another ice age, that million-and-a-half-
year period just before our own present, brought the
end of many of the older mammals, already far too set
in their ways. Some fled southward. Of those which remained in the inhospitable north, only the very hardy
ones survived, the ones that had warm coats and heft
and weight and an insulating layer of lard. And yet—
without such a coat, without appreciable size and
weight—the hardiest of all in his time was man.

EARLY HORSES

MAN AMONG THE VERTEBRATES
The House That Jack Built

If you were to think of our common human form as a sort of house, you could say that, in this house, man himself installed the telephone; that the electrical wiring was by courtesy of the primates; that mammals did the shingling and siding, the heating and the plumbing. But the foundation for the house was laid by the first vertebrates, perhaps 500 million years ago. To them we owe the basic underlying carpentry. Theirs is the shell, the frame, the plan. All the rest are frills and refinements.

The basic structure—stripped clean of its decoration—is bilaterally symmetrical, balanced, even on both sides. There are also two distinct ends, fore and aft. One end is usually capped with a skull containing a

THE VERTEBRATE PLAN   a water-living vertebrate

a land-living vertebrate

sensory switchboard of greater or lesser complexity, depending on the particular animal it serves. Also on the skull are two eyes, two sets of apparatus for hearing or balance or both, usually two nostrils, one mouth with (more often than not) teeth arranged for evenness of number. There are, amidships, two girdles to which are attached the paired limbs (or fins).

Inside the body there is a system for circulating blood—the simplest being merely a pulsating tube. (It is, incidentally, as a pulsating tube that our embryonic heart begins to beat.) The vertebrate plan (or better still, the chordate plan, so as to encompass our less complex relatives) also includes an apparatus for extracting oxygen from the environment—gills in sea animals, lungs for landlubbers. However, as was mentioned earlier, all dry-shod creatures repeat the gill stage in their embryonic lives.

Early chordates were probably segmented, with muscles arranged in a succession of identical blocks. This original segmentation is recalled in the higher forms by separate vertebral discs strung like beads down the back. And this brings us to the most outstanding of our group's common characteristics: that dorsal stiffening, the spine. Among early forms it appeared as a flexible rod of cartilage—the notochord—which kept segmentary bodies from collapsing on themselves like boy scout camping cups. Above the notochord in early chordates (and in simple living chordates still) was the nerve tube. Among the higher vertebrates this tube came to be enclosed within bony vertebrae, and the notochord disappeared. (It still turns up briefly during our embryonic careers to remind us of our heritage.)

Along with the stiffened bony spine came stiffened bony ribs and bony limbs as well. The vertebrate body is, in fact, entirely supported from within. No shells, no plates, no houses of horn for us (not for *most* of us, at any rate). This inner structure is one of great strength and flexibility. Because of it, animals could achieve large size and complex organization. Because of it, vertebrates could invade the land and, bereft of the sea's buoyancy, still withstand the pull of gravity. It permitted diversity of outer form and encouraged many variations on a theme. Not very surprisingly, various

ADAPTATION	SHALLOW-WATER LIFE	MARINE LIFE	WINGED FLIGHT	PROTECTIVE ARMOR
FISH		shark	flying fish	ostracoderm
REPTILE	duck-billed dinosaur	ichthyosaur	pterosaur	ankylosaur
BIRD	duck	penguin	gull	
MAMMAL	platypus	dolphin	bat	armadillo

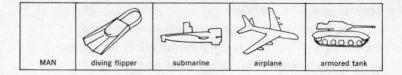

| MAN | diving flipper | submarine | airplane | armored tank |

types of vertebrates, all in possession of that flexible inner structure, evolved rather similar "solutions" to similar problems of environment and competition, such as webbed feet for swimming, wings for flight, and armored plate for defense.

Tempted by enterprise and curiosity, man ventured into every sort of environment occupied by his vertebrate kin and was there promptly confronted by the same problems and dangers. Instead of bodily adaptations, however, he depended on invention, on devices or machines, which would fit him for whatever new realms he chose to enter. And again, not very surprisingly, his manufactured adaptations closely imitate nature's biological ones.

The flexible vertebrate plan had to begin somewhere, of course, among simpler forms of life. Nearly all the invertebrate groups have been examined at one time or another in the hope of finding a potential ancestor. It seems now that our likeliest invertebrate relatives are to be found among creatures which look, at first glance, to be unlikeliest of all. Who would ever imagine that free-moving, active vertebrates could possibly have anything in common with starfishes or sea lilies? All those pointed arms radiating out from a middle certainly bear no resemblance whatever to our bilateral symmetry. But wait.

Scientists have discovered that the star shape is a secondary development in echinoderms ("spiny skins") and believe that their ancestors were once quite as bilateral as you or I. (Balance and a straightforward emphasis on the head region seem to have been a going trend long before chordates made an appearance. The common flatworm, for instance, is a headfirst individual, probably much older than the most primitive vertebrate.) The starfish's claim to bilateral symmetry is established in its larval form. What is more, the starfish larva is practically indistinguishable from the larvae of some of our own lower chordate relatives. And in chemical comparisons the body proteins of the two groups—echinoderms and lower chordates—show very marked similarities.

A clue as to how the transformation from a bristly appearance and sedentary habits to free-living mobility

might have come about can be found in the life story of
the lower chordates. Most of them look scarcely more
promising than the echinoderms. One group, the tuni-
cates, resemble nothing so much as immovable little
pitchers with two spouts. Again kinship is revealed in
the larvae. Young sea squirts, tiny and transparent, are
equipped with a complete notochord and nerve cord
just above it, a heart, a set of gills—all the rudiments
of "vertebratry." They are, moreover, free-swimming
until the day when, up-ended in the sand, they become
mere funnels, covered with a stiff mantle of secretions
—the tunic which gives the group its name.

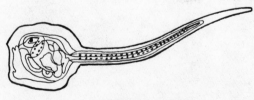

ADULT
SEA SQUIRTS

As the Canadian zoologist N. J. Berrill suggests,
some ancient sea squirts may have evolved the trick of
playing Peter Pan and kept his larval form for good.
Appendicularia, a tunicate relative, is a living example
of just such backwardness. He lives out his life, forever
refusing to grow up and settle down. Keep in mind this
"Peter Pan" concept. Scientists call it *neoteny;* we will
meet it again when we come to man.

The first orthodox chordate may have looked something like the lancelet, a tiny primitive animal alive
today. Its scientific name is *Amphioxus,* or "pointed at
both ends." And pointed it is, the better to burrow in
sandy sea bottoms where it often hides. Though it is
quite specialized for its sort of life, it does bear many
of the traits we might reasonably expect to find in a
vertebrate ancestor. It is segmented, has a notochord
and a nerve cord, and is gristly inside. It has a negligible

LARVAL SEA SQUIRT

mouth but plenty of gills, a great many more than any other chordate, living or extinct. Its brain is nothing much to speak of. Neither are its sensory organs. In place of eyes, it must make do with a pigmented spot placed strategically in front of its miniscule head. Its vertebrate house is unfurnished, slap-dash, incomplete; yet the plan is recognizably our own.

The oldest vertebrates with enough structural stiffening to fossilize and leave a record in the rocks were armored fishes, which first appeared perhaps 450 million years ago. Some scientists believe that early chordate ancestors migrated from the sea and did much of their evolving in fresh water. The development of elaborate armor may therefore have served as much to keep the necessary saltiness inside their bodies as to keep enemies out. They had no jaws, and their mouths were round suction cups with which they vacuumed the river bottoms. This sort of mouth relates them to living forms such as the jawless lamprey, scourge of freshwater lakes. It kills off game fish by clamping itself to them with its suction mouth, then rasping into their flesh and draining them dry of blood and juices.

LAMPREY'S MOUTH

Somewhere along the evolutionary line, fishes (armored still) acquired jaws. A fortunate migration of gill arches provided them, while external scales and plates functioned somewhat as teeth. These new jawed fishes became the terror of the deep. One called *Dinichthys,* "terrible fish"—and he deserves the name—was as much as 30 feet long. At the end of their heyday, these

LAMPREY

DINICHTHYS
the "terrible fish"

jawed and armored monsters shared the waters with two new sorts of fish. Both were fleet and free and relatively unarmored, though one was supported internally by a sub-structure of cartilage and the other by a skeleton of bone. Fish of the first type took up residence in the sea and there became ancestors to modern sharks and rays. From the bony fish—and specifically one group of bony fish—was to come all the vast parade of land vertebrates.

The bony fish themselves parted company soon after their first appearance to form two distinct groups. There were those with neat, elegant, raylike fins. Many members of this group would, during Mesozoic times, desert fresh water for the sea. And there were other bony fish of old-fashioned, conservative bent, whose fins were stumpy, awkward, lobelike.

Both the ray-finned fish and the lobe-fins were in possession of an odd little air sac connecting with their throats. This sac proved to be a very useful item during Devonian times (often called the Age of Fishes), about 405 million years ago. For a long time the climate was harsh and unsettled. Wet periods alternated with dry ones. Many waterways disappeared, and lakes shrank to ponds. Because of their air sacs, bony denizens of these brackish ponds could gulp enough extra oxygen to stay alive. In later times the air sacs of most sea-dwelling ray-finned fish would be converted to ballast organs, of no use at all in respiration.

The lobe-finned fish, however, found continued use for the air sac. One group of their relatives, the living African lungfish, still bound to an environment with alternating seasons of wetness and dryness, hibernate in the mud, utterly dependent on their auxiliary lungs. When the water returns, they break from their mud-walled prisons and become once again creatures of the gill. Ancient lobe-fins must have lived in much the same way, though perhaps without indulging in such long periods of hibernation. On their stumpy fins (many modern lungfishes now have less fins than tentacles), they perhaps crawled from one brackish pond to another in search of fresher water. And in following an old way of life, they evolved one which was altogether new.

Eventually, as creatures of the land, their descendants became amphibians. A very early one was *Ichthyostega*—still a bit more than halfway fish. The name, which means "fish-roof," describes its streamlined head.

Amphibians found a land already beginning to be clothed in pulpy treelike growths and populated by crawling scorpions and millipedes, probably the first creatures to leave the water home. The amphibian intruders soon assumed new forms, adopted new diets,

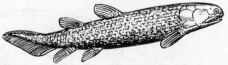

EARLY LOBE-FINNED FISH

acquired new habits. Some even grew monstrously large. One and all, however, they had this in common: they were still bound to the water. Only there could they get the moisture they periodically needed. Only there could their jelly-like eggs be fertilized and incubated. Only there could the fish-formed larvae, the tadpoles, live until their transformation to adulthood had been completed.

In another time of dryness and upheaval the water was left behind forever. It was not an adult pioneer who bridged the gap. It was her egg. The wonderful land egg was as decided an improvement in vertebrate propagation as mammalian live-birth was later to be. What it did was to bring the incubating water ashore, encased within a shell strong enough to protect the developing embryo, porous enough to let in oxygen and let out carbon dioxide. It contained a generous yolk and two special membranes: one which enfolded embryo and liquid, and one which introduced oxygen and received wastes. From such an egg, the infant creature could emerge fully formed, skipping the tadpole stage altogether.

With the land egg, reptiles were born. In the beginning they looked very like their amphibian forebears. But from this stem, what a branching forth! It spelled the end of the amphibian monopoly. Quickly they were reduced in number—eaten or driven by competition into corners where they remain today as frogs, toads, newts, and salamanders.

EARLY REPTILE

In spite of their dominance and quick proliferation, life was not all ease for early reptiles. Like the amphibians before them, they were not efficiently constructed for the demands of land living. There was, for instance, the matter of poor weight distribution. So much energy had to be expended in hoisting their heavy bodies off the ground and onto clumsy reptilian legs that little was left over for the necessary business of living. Some creatures never developed grace or speed at all and continued to look much like today's monitor lizard with his splayed-out limbs. Others found lightness and quickness in a return to the water. Phytosaurs and, later, crocodiles frequented shallow streams. Ichthyosaurs adapted completely to the sea environment and came to look much like modern dolphins. But the marine plesiosaurs rather resembled rowboats with paddles and must have been just about as speedy. Perhaps their long, snaky necks and darting heads compensated for their tubby hulls. Latest of all the marine reptiles were the frightful mosasaurs, which must have looked as close a thing to dragons as ever you will find outside a story book.

The response evolved by mammal-like reptiles to the pull of gravity was a trend toward tucking the legs neatly underneath the body. Among their descendants this trend would become more pronounced.

An altogether different stance "solved" the gravity problem for the ruling reptiles—the dinosaurs. Characteristic of them is the tripod posture: a rearing back on

TYRANNOSAURUS

two hind legs and a tail. In time the front limbs of many upright ruling reptiles degenerated until they became mere appendages, and pretty useless ones at that. *Tyrannosaurus rex,* the familiar "tyrant king" of the end of the Age of Dinosaurs, had just such shriveled forepaws.

Many plant-eating dinosaurs became so ponderously heavy that they reassumed the four-legged posture. But their hips and hind legs—so much larger than the limbs up front—testified to former stances and earlier days.

Beyond the problem of size and stance, there was also the matter of temperature regulation. It became increasingly important as the climates shifted and changed. Two sets of reptile offshoots evolved solutions. The mammals, as we have seen, were one; birds were the other.

PLANT-EATING BRONTOSAURUS

THE REPTILE FAMILY

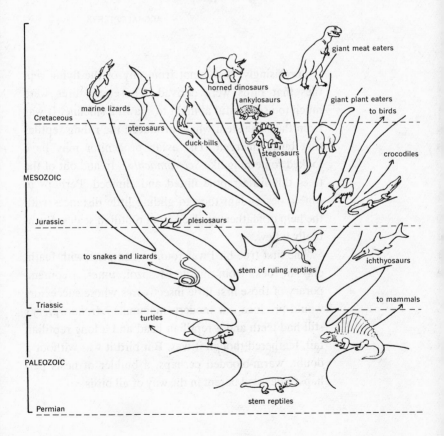

ARCHAEOPTERYX

Surprisingly, it was not from any of the flying reptiles that birds were derived. Those creatures were
much too successful at flight to spawn a sideline. It was
from the same stem which produced the ruling reptiles
that birds emerged. The avian progenitor may have
looked something like *Scleromochlus*. In and out of the
trees this little reptile flitted and climbed. Perhaps in
time a descendant took to gliding little distances with
the help of feathers evolved from reptilian scales. Eventually it flew.

The first true bird was found—complete with feathers—in rocks from middle Mesozoic times, a contem-
porary of those first little insectivores whose successors
would produce our modern mammals. *Archaeopteryx*
still had teeth and a reptilian head and a long reptilian
tail, feathered though it was. But bird it was without a
doubt, warm-blooded perhaps, a builder of nests perhaps, a devoted parent in the way of all birds.

By the time the Age of Recent Life rolled around, birds had assumed a multitude of sizes and shapes. In some places where mammals had not yet produced forms of respectable strength, birds themselves became predators, huge and truly terrible.

Birds today are a far cry from their reptilian past. And yet, when you look at a bluejay's checkered coat, sometimes you can almost see the pattern of scales underneath the feathers—dark blues and light blues and grays overlapping in tiny plates. And for a moment you foolishly look for teeth that have long since disappeared, a drooping tail, a slither instead of a hop.

Now we have met all our vertebrate tribe: fish, amphibians, reptiles, mammals, and birds—all with the same inner structure, the same foundation; all in the house that some unknown Jack built—some tunicate Jack, perhaps, some starfish Jack—long, long ago.

5

MAN AMONG MEN
A Hominid Who's Who

When it comes to man one thing is certain: we are older than we think.

For a long time we have seen our kind as fairly recent arrivals, new-rich upstarts among the staid old hominoids. Even the most generous guesses have not, until recently, given us more than a million years of tenure as hominids. (I suppose you could say that *-id* is to *-oid* as *-ish* is to *-like*. *Mannish* is more so than *manlike* and *hominid* more than *hominoid*.) Since the hominoids as a group date back at least 25 million years, many authorities have wondered how we came by our own trademarks so quickly. (In the long view, a million years is "quickly.") What sort of environment favored the development of the human face and

form—our upright posture insured by an ample pelvis
and double-curved spine, our small teeth, our smooth
faces with their jutting noses and chins? For all of these
features are radically different from those of our
cousins, the great apes, long presumed to represent the
main line of hominoid descent.

"It was the move from trees to ground," some specialists say. "Tall savannah grasses hid predators, and
whichever beginning man could stand tallest and see
most had the advantage. In time erect posture developed."

"Oh, no," others maintained, "it was because, once
on the ground, man became a carrier. He carried rocks
to throw at lions. He carried meat away from some
other animal's kill. Without pockets, he had to use his
hands. And the individual whose hands were freed by
upright posture had the edge."

"You see," say a third group, "beginning man was
already a tool user, and that accounts for his small size
and modest teeth. While other ground-living primates
acquired large size and developed their fangs for defense, man protected himself with rocks and sticks and
bones."

"He's a domestic animal," adds another. "He tamed
himself. Domesticated animals are always smaller,
lighter, smoother-boned than wild ones. That's what
happened in time to man."

"Love did it," sigh still others. "Females liked their
menfolk to look a certain way, and vice versa. People

CHIMP CARRYING BANANAS

with the popular sort of face and form got mates while everyone else stayed single."

"It wasn't love at all; it was neoteny," insist a different group. "Man is an ape that never grew up. Look how similar our skulls are to those of young gorillas. It's only later that the ape's bony superstructure appears, and hair, too. We skipped this later stage, that's all—we stayed younger longer and were able to learn more."

INFANT GORILLA

Very likely all these suggested environmental pressures and growth mechanisms, and even individual preferences, played a part in shaping our form and frame. And then again there may be another answer. Or, at least, an additional one. Perhaps our physical type simply harks back to the original line of hominoid development. Perhaps it is not we who are newcomers on the scene, but the others instead. Certainly we seem to be in some ways more conservative than our cousins the apes. We have, for instance, a greater number of lower vertebrae than they do and therefore more of a "tail." Our shorter arms and longer thumbs may follow the old pattern more faithfully than long, brachiating arms and shorter thumbs. And certainly features such as modest teeth and smooth faces seem to go back a long, long way. At least one member of the dryopithecine complex (a varied and long-lived group of hominoids which included ancestors of living great apes and of early man) was not at all beetle-browed. He has been named *Proconsul,* and he dates back perhaps 24

ADULT GORILLA

ADULT MAN

million years. Others of this group were quite as fang-less as we. The jaw fragment of one such hominoid—discovered during 1962 in Kenya, East Africa, and called (appropriately enough) *Kenyapithecus*—shows something else besides. Above the canine tooth there is a little indentation in the bone. Such a cavity in man is called a canine fossa, and it is not found in living apes. On it is anchored a muscle which has to do with lip movements in speech. As the British anthropologist Dr. L. S. B. Leakey (the fossil's discoverer) has pointed out, this does not mean that *Kenyapithecus* could speak, but he had that potential. His age has been estimated at 14 million years. We do not know whether he was directly ancestral to our kind, but he was cer-tainly close to creatures who were.

Unfortunately nothing has yet been found of this fossil hominoid but his teeth. (Remains similar to his have also been found in India.) Teeth cannot tell of the progress toward upright posture. And certainly a change in posture preceded the expansion in brain size so characteristic of later man. Teeth do not tell us, either, just why, having taken to ground life, we evolved toward brains instead of brawn. The absence of fangs suggests that artificial means of defense had been found, but that is all. Nonetheless, these fossils do indicate that our line (or something near it) is very, very old and that our pedigree is every bit as long as that of any other hominoid.

From all our direct evidence, we can say only these

few things for sure. We did at some time become land instead of tree dwellers. We did stay small and pliable. We did change our diet from mostly vegetable to mostly meat. We did become tool users and, eventually, tool makers. And somewhere along the line, we were thrust into a wholly different plane of life. It was a life in which hunting had replaced gathering, and speech had replaced signals. There were families as well as bands and, eventually, tradition, rituals, and social order. As we will see in later chapters, this new way of life seemed to set up its own pressures, selecting for individuals with ever-better brains—individuals who could hunt better, raise smarter children, influence others, and deal with ideas. As man's brain power increased, so did his capacity for cultural invention, until at length his symbols and his society became his environment and his humanity. Exactly when each of these steps occurred and how they came about, we still do not know.

Actually, we have only recently begun to think about ourselves in terms of our evolutionary development. Such thinking picked up speed with the publication of Charles Darwin's books, *On the Origin of Species* (1859) and, later, *The Descent of Man*. Then came the discoveries of fossil men. As you might expect, the most recent in time were the first uncovered. Every decade or so since has seen our notions of man's antiquity pushed back, until now we have passed the million-year mark and are well on our way to two.

The first of our ancient men turned up in a cave above a peaceful little German valley, Neanderthal by name. Many prominent anatomists and other men of science insisted the bones were those of some unfortunate fellow who had crawled in there to die. His prow-nosed, chinless face, his flat-topped head, his legs, so short and grotesquely bowed, were chalked up to rheumatism or possibly rickets, poor old soul!

At this time (Darwin's first book was soon to be published) strange animal fossils were thought to represent life forms which had existed before each of several great floods. It was believed that after each of these catastrophes, life had been created anew, sometimes in forms wildly different from those of preceding populations. Humanity was supposed to have begun only after the final catastrophe, which many likened to the Biblical deluge. The notion that the man of Neanderthal could possibly be older than Noah's flood was unthinkable. In time, however, and with accumulating skeletons—all with the same "deformities" and all found with "pre-deluge" animal bones—the unthinkable had to be thought. Neanderthal Man was very, very old—older than man's Creation.

With this realization, general opinion shifted violently into reverse. If this Neanderthal creature really was as old as all that, then better not to think of him as human at all. And the picture of a poor old rheumatic vagrant was replaced with that of a hulking ape, a sort of "missing link."

It was not until later, when even older fossil men

NEANDERTHAL MAN

began to be uncovered, that Neanderthal Man was gradually reaccepted into the ranks of humanity. Nowadays he is considered a member not only of our genus (*Homo*), but of our species (*sapiens*) as well. His brain was certainly as large as, if not larger than, our own. And his stubby body and other oddities are thought by many specialists to reflect nothing more than adaptations to the cold climate in which he lived. At most he is considered a subspecies, or perhaps a racial type. If one of his modern reconstructions were to come to life, like Pygmalion's statue, you probably wouldn't give him a second glance in a crowd—assuming, of course, that he had been given a tweed suit instead of a pelt to wear.

Next in point of discovery—midway in point of hominid development—was *Homo erectus,* Upright Man. The first representative of this group to be unearthed, however, was not called Man at all but Upright Ape Man—*Pithecanthropus erectus*. His discoverer, the Dutch doctor Eugen Dubois, was one of the luckiest men ever to dig for scientific treasure. He went to Java in 1898 with the express hope of finding a fossil hominid, and sure enough, he did just that.

What an uproar broke out when *Pithecanthropus* was unveiled. Surely, many people thought, here was a creature more ape than human—a real "missing link." And it was as an ape that *Pithecanthropus* was most often pictured. For, although a skeleton can be reconstructed from pieces, and although those pieces show where and how muscles were attached in life, they tell

PITHECANTHROPUS
(more ape than man)

nothing about hair and skin and wrinkles and facial
expression. This must remain a matter of artist's choice.
And his choice is likely to reflect current feeling as
much as anything else.

Eventually, more and more Upright Ape Men were
discovered, and in many parts of the world (our hemisphere excepted). Most were found with patterned
tools, some with the remains of fire. And when careful
skull measurements were taken and comparisons made,
the realization dawned that, while Upright Ape Men had
not been geniuses, their brains were still a good deal
larger than ape brains and not very much smaller than
the brains of some living *Homo sapiens*. The concep-
tion of our hominid age had by now stretched to include the half-million-year mark, when Upright Man
had flourished. Obviously our ancestors were older still.
Homo erectus was, after all, no "missing link."

In the early 1920s, fossil creatures still more primitive than *Pithecanthropus* turned up in South Africa.
Their discoverer, the British scientist Dr. Raymond A.
Dart, called them collectively australopithecines—
southern apes. Judging by the animal bones he found
with them, he thought they might be as much as a
million years old. "Ah," breathed an interested public,
"*here* is the missing link."

From the first, however, Dr. Dart insisted that his
discoveries had made tools—perhaps of stone, and certainly of bone. With antelope thigh bones for clubs, he
thought, the australopithecines had combatted their

PITHECANTHROPUS
(more man than ape)

enemies and killed their prey. Long split bones had
served as knives. He even claimed for one of his finds
the knowledge of fire and promptly named him *Aus-
tralopithecus prometheus,* after the legendary bringer
of fire from the gods. The scientific world did not agree
and refused to consider the australopithecines as anything higher than near-men or man-apes, erect stand-
ing, perhaps, but small brained and toolless.

And so the matter stood until 1959. In that year, Dr.
Leakey and his wife unearthed *Zinjanthropus.*

For many years the Leakeys had spent their free time
searching the East African countryside for relics of
man's past. They had scoured areas around, and islands
in, Lake Victoria and in 1948 had been rewarded with
Proconsul. Most promising of all the sites, they had
long thought, was Olduvai Gorge in Tanganyika. An
area which, in its past, had been alternately lake and
desert, it was in time eroded away to expose the layers
of ancient soil deposits. Near the bottom of these layers
was found a hominid skull, the remains of a camp site,
and many pebble tools. By 1959 better methods of
dating antiquities had been perfected. Since radioactive
elements decay at given rates, it is possible to tell when
rock containing these elements was laid down by meas-
uring how much of them remains. Tests of the volcanic
rock covering the fossil show it to have been deposited
close to 1,750,000 years ago. It is likely that the bones,
too, are that old.

Dr. Leakey called his fossil *Zinjanthropus*—East

African Man. In view of Zinj's apparent ability with tools, popular imagination veered quite away from any suggestion of apehood. Early reconstructions showed him as a noble savage, a bit low of brow but recognizably human.

In time there was a general settling down. It was agreed that Zinj was, after all, quite definitely related to the australopithecines down south and that the whole group would have to be promoted from man-apes to something next door to humanity if not in the same house.

Now a rough evolutionary progression began to be outlined. There had been, it appeared, three distinct, increasingly complex levels of development through which mankind had passed on its way to *Homo sapiens:* the dryopithecine stage—the time of proto-men, whoever and whatever they were; the australopithecine stage, with the rough beginnings of tool making; and the *erectus* stage, in which men were Men (though primitively so), with more sophisticated tools, fire, and probably other elements of culture as well.

The whole picture has recently been considerably enriched by another Leakey discovery. In a level a little beneath the one which contained *Zinjanthropus* (and therefore of even earlier date) were found the remains

TWO RECONSTRUCTIONS OF ZINJANTHROPUS

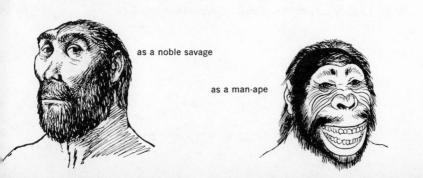

as a noble savage

as a man-ape

of men very much more like ourselves than any of the australopithecines. These men were definitely tool makers, rock-shelter makers, perhaps real hunters. *Homo habilis*—Man (definitely man) the skillful—Dr. Leakey named this discovery, of whom no reconstructions have as yet been published. Here, then, was true man living concurrently with what had been thought to be his forerunner. Some authorities, including Dr. Leakey himself, have begun to doubt whether Zinj's tools were really his own after all. Perhaps they had been made by the new men instead.

Where does this leave us? If Zinj and the australopithecines represent an offshoot, not directly ancestral to true man, just how old are we? A lot older than we have thought, certainly. Our beginnings have been pushed back yet again, deep into that thirteen-million-year blank spot between *Kenyapithecus* and his kind, and the time when *Homo habilis* lived and thrived. There is, it would seem, no one "missing link" but many. A good deal more digging remains to be done before our genealogy is complete.

The generally accepted way of sorting out relationships among the apes, the fossil men, and ourselves (excluding *Homo habilis* for now) looks something like this:

HOMINOIDS	HOMINIDS	HOMININES (True Men)
Living great apes		
Gibbons and ancestors		
Dryopithecine apes		
Australopithecines	Australopithecines	
Homo erectus	*Homo erectus*	*Homo erectus*
Homo sapiens	*Homo sapiens*	*Homo sapiens*

The *hominine,* or true man, category is occupied only by *Homo erectus* and *Homo sapiens*—Man the Wise—ourselves. And since *erectus* types have long since disappeared, you might say it belongs to us alone.

No one knows for sure just where the first *sapiens* individuals came from or when they appeared. The earliest fossils to be given even possible *sapiens* status were found in Swanscombe, England, and Steinheim, Germany. They date back perhaps 300,000 years or so, and their thickened skulls suggest a rather recent emergence from *erectus* stock, or perhaps connections with the Neanderthalers, who, nevertheless, did not turn up in strength until some time later.

STEINHEIM SKULL

Doubtless Miss Swanscombe and Miss Steinheim (the skulls are thought to have belonged quite definitely to ladies) were oddities even among their *erectus* peers. Doubtless they would not be considered beauties in our world, either. But their descendants in time replaced *Homo erectus* all over the world just as he had replaced the australopithecines. By the end of the last glacial period, even the sapient Neanderthalers—so different in their squat way from the rest of the group—had been hustled off the stage. *Homo sapiens sapiens* (a convenience term; we're not really doubly wise) came into his own.

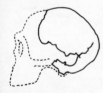

SWANSCOMBE SKULL
(dotted lines show
a reconstruction)

What happened to these various kinds of men whose day on earth so suddenly came to an end? The popular picture has conjured up scenes of battle. Especially in the case of *Homo sapiens neanderthalensis* vs. *Homo sapiens sapiens* has this image been employed: a sort of prehistoric cops and robbers game—the hulking bad guys against the clean-limbed, clear-eyed good guys. Hurray for our side!

But things may not have happened that way at all. Peoples have vanished as entities even in historic times, and though some were exterminated in the bad old way, others were simply absorbed into the dominant group around them. This may have happened with the Neanderthalers.

As for the simpler types of men, perhaps it was not so much a matter of being overrun and replaced as of growing up. All over the world, subject to the pressures of an ever more complicated life, Upright Man may slowly have evolved into Sapient Man. Perhaps he took with him into the new estate his local differences of skin color, shape of eye, length of leg—all thought to be adaptations to varying climates and regions. However he came to be, mankind was then and is now *one*—a single species of tremendous flexibility and variety, of possibilities and potentialities.

We need this variety to draw on. For we have not stopped evolving, and we shall not, so long as human life lasts. Judging by the dominant trend of our past, we should be moving still toward better brains, if not bigger ones. Infant skulls are already about as big as they conveniently can be for birth, so we cannot look to size for improvement. Another excursion into neoteny might help us to stay young longer and keep our skulls

HOMO SAPIENS
NEANDERTHALENSIS

growing. In the long run, perhaps we will simply have to do more with the brain size we already have. Certainly the environment still favors intelligence and will continue to do so.

But this environment we have created is selecting for a great many other traits in addition to intelligence. The machines we have invented to make our lives comfortable, to transport us at high speeds, and to make more and more goods for us to use—these machines are filling our air with wastes often downright poisonous to breathe. The discovery of atomic power has given us both friend and enemy. For the effects of too much exposure to radiation (whether from fallout after weapons tests or from the familiar x-ray machine) are long-lasting and dangerous, not only to living individuals, but to generations yet unborn. Our planet grows thick with people jostling, crowding, irritating each other. If the trend continues unchecked, we shall soon have little living room left.

It is easy to see how human mutants able to withstand dirty air, radioactivity, crowding, and stress would certainly have an edge over us "normal" folk. If these new abilities just happened to be housed in bodies even slightly different from the present type, it would not take long for a permanent shift in human looks to take place. In time our descendants might resemble us so little as to rate a different name altogether. Perhaps it might be something like *Homo supervivens*—Man the Survivor. At that point *Homo sapiens,* replaced and succeeded, would be just another museum exhibit.

In terms of time, we have only just started on our way. Not yet have we begun to approach the dinosaurs' span or even that of the common opossum, whose kind has existed for over sixty million years. If we can somehow manage to hang on, to solve the problems we ourselves have created, to be ever more, instead of ever less, human, we might yet enter another world of wonders—as different from our present world as was the way of humanity for our ancestors in their dim beginning.

FROM THE BEGINNING

A MINUTE = 75 MILLION YEARS
THE HOUR = 4.5 BILLION YEARS

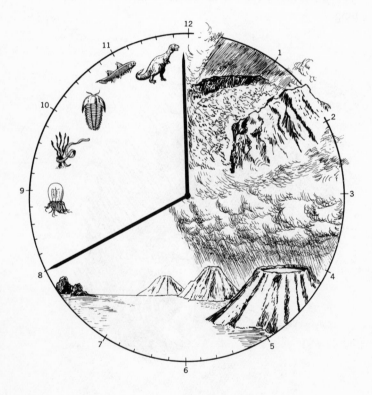

6

MAN IN TIME
Clocks of Ages

Have you ever tried to think of TIME? Not the yesterday, today, and tomorrow in which our lives unfold.
Not last year, already growing dim in memory. Not
even the last hundred years, lost to our immediate
knowledge except as it exists in written history. Not a
thousand years or a million, but ALL TIME since time
began. For us, time begins with the earth's beginning.
Beyond is the time when time was not: infinity, eternity
—before the thought of which our time-bound human
minds balk, refusing us a picture. Eternity remains a
word.

To think back to the earth's beginning is surely task
enough. What are billions to us, be it dollars or years?
Numbers in a national budget, dates on a scientific
chart—quantities so huge as to be almost unimagi-
nable. And nature's time clocks—the slowly decaying

radioactive materials of our earth—tell us that the oldest known rocks were formed more than three billion
years ago. Meteorites dating from the birth of the solar
system are even older—at least four and a half billion
years. This is now thought to be the minimum age of
our planet as well. Some scientists, however, speak of
six billion as a likelier age for old Earth and her sister
planets, and even this starting point may soon be
shoved backward into the past. And what is that to us,
the talk of billions, one or many? Words still.

But let us take what the meteorites tell us of earth
time and what the rocks and the fossils of once living
things have to say and reduce their story to the minutes
of one mortal hour. Let's choose the hour between
eleven and twelve and make each minute worth 75 million years.

A MINUTE = 75 MILLION YEARS

THE HOUR = 4.5 BILLION YEARS

FROM THE BEGINNING

As the hour strikes, young Earth is still a whirling, formless mass. Its own crust, its own rocks have not yet begun to form.

11:00

The oldest of Earth's rocks are in formation. In the minutes following, Earth's crust forms and slowly cools. The only atmosphere is a poisonous one, dense with the water vapors and fumes poured forth from countless volcanoes. Hot lava sears the cooling crust. Gases gradually collect and condense. Drenching rains fall, and from their waters shallow seas begin to form. Soupy seas, they are, rich in chemicals and possibility. Periodically the murk is pierced by lightning, bombarded by cosmic rays. Either or perhaps both spark the chemical processes which lead to the formation of organic compounds, the building blocks of life.

11:10

Earth's crust buckles as it cools, heaving up bare wastes of land above the waters. In the warm seas, or perhaps in deep volcanic pools (first bubbling hot, then cool), the building blocks assemble in ever more complex forms until at length the first cell-like structures appear and, with them, Life.

11:24   Cells are developing rapidly. The remains of blue-green algae dating from this time show that a good deal of complexity had already been achieved in cellular life. The fast-multiplying plant cells give off the oxygen which, with carbon dioxide, becomes part of the earth's atmosphere. Mutant cells able to use oxygen in their metabolism become the first animals.

11:44   Cells have by now joined into cooperative colonies, soft, yielding, and probably transparent. (Only a few imprints of primitive jellyfish and the streaky burrows of worms remain to suggest the forms of developing life.)

11:52   Sea-bottom life at last appears in quantity and variety and leaves us its remains.

11:55   Animals invade the land.

11:59¼   Mammals appear.

And where in these last few moments are we? Our whole time on earth occupies little more than a second of this hour, appearing just as the clock strikes twelve.

But let us take the last twenty minutes of this hour and expand them into an hour all their own, an hour in which each minute will be worth 25 million years. Perhaps then we can see how we fit in.

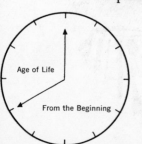

Age of Life

From the Beginning

THE AGE OF LIFE

A MINUTE = 25 MILLION YEARS
THE HOUR = 1.5 BILLION YEARS

Life is already well organized at the cellular level   11:00
and developing rapidly.

Some one-celled creatures have developed hard cov-   11:15
erings. Cooperative colonies of cells appear—something, perhaps, like modern *Volvox* (the dotted globes

shown) or like red algae, the feathery sea moss of today. Colonies specialize, turn up as tissue layers in still
more complex creatures: sponges, for instance. With
still finer specialization, there appear animals having
nerve nets (the hydra and jellyfish) and internal organs
(flatworms). All, however, are soft-bodied and leave
few traces in the shifting sea sands.

11:36
CAMBRIAN

Animals with shells and stiffened exteriors are suddenly everywhere. Some are clamlike, others rather resemble today's horseshoe crabs. These are the trilobites, which will dominate undersea life for nearly ten
minutes. The greenery of sea plants enlivens the scene.
Some of them will precede animals to the shore.

11:40
ORDOVICIAN

There are still more varieties of sea life: giant snails
and tentacled nautiloids, sea scorpions and starfish, and
still a quantity of trilobites. The first recognizable vertebrates appear in fresh-water rivers and lakes. No one
is yet sure of their ultimate ancestry. They are stiffened
inside by a framework of gristle, outside (like their
invertebrate peers) with a suit of armor. They are jawless, sweepers of muddy bottoms, fishlike in appearance.

SILURIAN 11:43

Many more fishlike creatures now appear. Though
armored still, all are jawed and provided with teeth.
Plants begin their invasion of the barren land. Already

the shores are dotted with spikey browns and greens. Soon after, scorpions and millipedes venture out of the water.

Two new sorts of fish turn up among the armored swimmers. One much resembles modern sharks and soon moves down the rivers and into the sea. The other group is composed of fish with true bones and air sacs, supplementary respirators during this time of mountain building, drying ponds, and torrential downpours. In some of the bony fish the air sac will become a land lung. In the others it will be converted into a ballast organ.

11:44 DEVONIAN

Some of the lungfishes—particularly those with stumpy, lobelike fins—begin to drag themselves from one brackish pond to another. In time their descendants become adapted to a life that is mostly out of water. They look something like *Ichthyostega,* half in, half out of the water. These new amphibians, emancipated though they are, still must return to the water to breed.

In the following moments, one group of amphibians comes to live on land altogether, for they have begun to lay eggs with hard shells—eggs containing miniature aquariums in which the young can develop quite independently of the incubating pond waters. These first reptiles may look something like *Seymouria,* shown leaving its cache of eggs. It looks to be part lizard, part salamander.

11:46½ CARBONIFEROUS

In the 2½ minutes of this period, great forests of pulpy, fernlike trees flourish in the humid air and die and sink into the swamps. From the rot of this primitive vegetation the earth's great coal deposits will be formed to give this time-span its name: Carboniferous —coal-bearing.

PERMIAN   11:49   Again the earth's crust buckles and heaves. The air grows cold. Glaciers appear over parts of the earth. A new type of reptile emerges, one seemingly better adapted to the violent changes than the older stem reptiles and the dwindling amphibians. These new reptiles

are the pelycosaurs—represented here by the finned-back *Dimetrodon,* a fierce, dominant predator. Its varied teeth and much of its bony structure show it to be on the line which will one day lead to mammals.

TRIASSIC   11:51   The Appalachian Mountains are formed in another great uplift ending the time of Old Life, or Paleozoic, forms and signaling the appearance of the time of Mesozoic, or Middle Life. The pelycosaurs die out and

are replaced by lighter, swifter reptiles, even more mammal-like than their predecessors. *Cynognathus* looks to be part lizard, part dog.

The true reptiles eventually reassert their ancient supremacy. Some, such as *Ichthyosaurus,* return to the sea and become so closely adapted to the new environment as to resemble fish. Other marine forms are on

the way. Short-legged *Nothosaurus* is to be ancestor to the later, long-necked *Plesiosaurus*. The first of the ruling reptile appears, already running on two legs as the graceful *Coelophysis* is doing. Though birdlike in appearance, it is eight feet long and a meat eater. By the end of this period, it and its cousins will have edged the mammal-like reptiles off the scene.

More mountains are formed and a new period be- gins. Reptiles now take to the air on leathery wings. By the next period, some will be the size of dragons— thirty feet from wing tip to wing tip. At 11:53 the first birds, arisen separately from a little reptile ancestor, also begin to fly. The first of the huge plant-eating dinosaurs, pushed onto all fours by expanding bulk, roam the marshland. *Stegosaurus* with its plated back is one. *Brontosaurus*—"thunder lizard"—is another, the largest land monster of all time. They are pursued by large meat eaters.

Watching warily are the first little mammals, already in four varieties. One will play ancestor to later, truer mammals, both marsupial and placental. Their furry coats protect them from cold and heat so that, unlike the dinosaurs, they are active in any weather. Perhaps they have already begun to bear their young alive instead of laying eggs. Or perhaps, like the living platypus, they still lay eggs but protect and care for the hatched young. Certainly they provide milk for their babies and teach them. And they do have bigger brains in proportion to their size than do the heedless dinosaurs, whose wits are so slow they need an extra brain in their tails.

11:55
CRETACEOUS

The meat-eating dinosaurs reach their most gigantic dimensions in *Tyrannosaurus,* who now is faced by *Triceratops,* a powerful, horned plant eater that somewhat resembles a rhinoceros.

Looking on is a still more advanced little mammal, something like a modern shrew or hedgehog. It is a placental mammal, but there are successful marsupials too, mostly ancestors of the modern opossum. All mammals of this period live primarily in trees, which by now include hardwood types, such as oaks, and flowering types such as magnolia, dogwood, and laurel.

With still another great continental uplift—in which the Alps and the Rocky Mountains have their beginning—the great dinosaurs mysteriously vacate the earth. Only snakes, turtles, lizards, crocodiles, and a few amphibians remain to give witness to its former rulers. Their successors, the mammals (represented here by *Plesiadapis,* a very early primate), inherit the earth.

11:57½
CENOZOIC ERA

Of that last 2½ minutes, man occupies only the last four or five seconds, too fleeting to be noticed or shown.

Suppose we take the time of mammals, all 63 million years of it, and give it an hour of its own. In this hour, each minute will be worth a touch over a million years —50 thousand, to be exact. To make it easy, let's just say a million years *plus*.

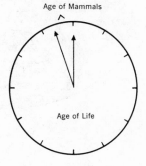

Age of Mammals

Age of Life

THE AGE OF MAMMALS

A MINUTE = 1 MILLION YEARS
THE HOUR = 63 MILLION YEARS

As the hour strikes, the land is stilled, the climate mild. Mammals have already begun to spread out and occupy the earth's living rooms. Many come down from the trees and begin to eat fruit, grass, and leaves instead of their former insect diet. Some of these new herbivores grow large and lumbering like *Barylambda,* who stood perhaps four feet at the shoulders. Already its clawed toes are beginning to suggest small hooves.

11:00   PALEOCENE

Some mammals acquire a taste for herbivores. They begin to play the role in life once taken by the meat-eating dinosaurs. *Loxolophus,* here preparing to spring at his much larger prey, is one such carnivore. In this early period, mammals were, for the most part, clumsy compared to their agile descendants, unsettled as to form and way of life. It is, all in all, a time of transition, of experimentation, and very often carnivores look like the animals they are hunting—and vice versa.

Still in the trees are the first primates. *Plesiadapis* lives during these five minutes, doing its best to compete with the growing tribe of rodents. A more generalized prosimian is the ancestor of today's tree shrew. At the other end of the vine an early opposum, *Didelphis,* hangs by its tail. It is, perhaps, the oldest of the marsupials and the only one to compete successfully and on a wide scale with the placental mammals.

During the next twenty minutes, the climate continues mild, and the jungle growths are lush and green.
Warm seas still dominate the globe. In them great
whales are already sporting. The air is divided by the
daytime birds and the nighttime bats.

The old animal forms are brought to their highest
development. The uintatheres are the largest of the
early hooved grass-eating animals. Like the great beast
wading in the pond, each is protected by six horns *and*
a pair of fangs. Dawn Horse—*Eohippus*—appears.
About the size of a fox terrier it is, still with many of
its toes—four on the front feet, three behind—each
capped by a tiny hoof.

One of its number has been killed by *Oxyaena,* a
dominant member of the old-fashioned carnivores. At
the end of the period, more modern sorts of carnivores
begin to appear. *Cynodictis* (perched on a background
rock) is one. It is, perhaps, an ancestor of the dog family.

The primates, which have remained in their ancient
home, are producing still more advanced types. *Noth-
arctus,* an early lemur, has appeared and also *Necro-
lemur,* perhaps the first tarsier, already with big, round,
nighttime eyes and a real face instead of a snout.

Change is in the air. Newer sorts of mammals appear, many of them foreshadowing modern types. Some of these are shown together in a mythical Oligocene landscape, and not in their native homes or with their natural companions. Of the old carnivores, only *Hyaenodon* remains. It is shown here chasing *Mesohippus,* a sheep-sized horse with three toes on each foot. The middle toe is by now much larger than the rest and bears most of the animal's body weight.

In the distance can be seen a gigantic *Baluchitherium* munching thoughtfully on a treetop. It is not only the biggest of all the rhinos, but the biggest land mammal ever, being eighteen feet high at the shoulders—a real giant. It is without a horn and doesn't need it. Its size is its protection.

In front of it is an even more rhinoceros-like animal who is, nevertheless, not a rhinoceros. Its feet are odd-toed, hooved, and its weight—like that of the horse (a close cousin)—rests on its middle toe. This huge creature is a titanothere—by name, *Brontops.*

Watching the scene are two new primates: an early Old World monkey (perhaps a creature like *Oligopithecus*) and a generalized hominoid like *Propliopithecus,* who lives partly in, partly out of the trees. Not yet has he developed the long arms characteristic of later brachiators. Some things about him are partly monkey-like, partly apelike, and partly human-like. He may be on or near the line that was to produce both apes and men.

MIOCENE 11:35

The weather is growing cooler and drier. Grasses flourish in the sun and spread out in widening meadows. All the hooved animals prosper in this setting. *Merychippus,* the Miocene horse, is as big now as a small pony. It still has three toes on each foot but does all its walking on the middle one only. The others are almost vestiges.

Related to it is the ungainly *Moropus,* whose three-toed feet bear claws instead of hooves. Perhaps it digs up roots with them, disdaining a grassy diet. A short-legged, two-horned rhinoceros surveys the scene. So does a piglike creature as big as a bison. Actually it is not a pig at all in spite of its looks. Its name is *Dinohyus.*

On the horizon two tall *Alticameli* with heads ten feet in the air run before *Machairodus,* one of the saber-toothed cats.

Looking on are two advancing hominoids, both members of a very large group of roughly similar types spread out all through the Old World during this period, shown here with animals from other continents.

Climbing the rocks is *Proconsul,* perhaps a likely ancestor for modern gorillas and chimpanzees. The squatting creature is *Kenyapithecus,* who may already be on the road to man. His sort appear at the end of the period or early in the next. There we lose track of him and his descendants.

The cold is coming. Winter—longer now century by century—alternates with summer. Trees turn red and lose their leaves. Many of the older animals are replaced by newer types, even more modern in form. The elephant family which began in the early Oligocene is now, in the early part of this period, approaching its ultimate size and weight. Such is the lumbering *Trilophodon,* whose lower lip projects almost as far forward as its prehensile nose.

The horse of the time, *Pliohippus,* is of nearly modern size. Already its side toes are concealed beneath the skin.

Tomarctus, direct ancestor of modern dogs, chases a deerlike creature with a bizarre horn on the end of its nose.

11:47   PLIOCENE

At the end of the period, concluded by another up-lift of the Rocky Mountains, winter arrives in all its cruel majesty. Ice is beginning to creep over the northern landscapes. Only the largest and hairiest of the northern mammals survive the change—animals such as the huge woolly mammoth, the woolly rhino, the cave bear, the woolly bison, and the giant sloth.

11:58½
PLEISTOCENE

And in this time of trial and change, man appears. Let us give him a clock of his own, watch his many faces, move with him through a world in which he had to use his brain to survive. Every minute on his clock is worth 25 thousand years.

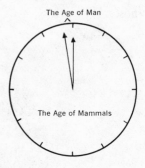

The Age of Man

The Age of Mammals

THE AGE OF MAN

A MINUTE = 25,000 YEARS
THE HOUR = 1.5 MILLION YEARS

As the hour begins, man—toolmaker, hunter, rock- 11:00
shelter builder—is already on the scene. No one can
say as yet how long he has been there or whence he

came. He is small, to be sure, and primitive. But he is recognizably one of our kind—true man. (He is represented here in dotted outline only, for his discovery has been too recent for scientists and artists to have reconstructed his likeness.) His discoverer calls him *Homo habilis*—man the skillful, able man.

Sharing the stage at 11:00 is another kind of man, different from *Homo habilis,* larger, cruder, more ape-like, an eater of rough vegetable foods and slow, easily caught game. He is *Zinjanthropus,* East African Man. His remains have been found in association with tools —tools, however, that may have been made and used, not by himself, but by his smaller neighbor, *Homo habilis.*

The African climate at 11:00 is a rainy one, and the landscape is lush and marshy. Far away up north the first of the great glaciers has taken much of Eurasia, much of North America in its icy grip.

11:30   All during the first half-hour *Zinjanthropus* and his relatives rule the African roost. They come in assorted sizes, some big, some little. Altogether they are called the australopithecines—the southern apes. Although they are upright in posture and may have made simple tools, their brains are not much bigger than those of gorillas.

Evidences of *Homo habilis* are few and puzzling, but he apparently survives to move on to better things.

True man again appears, this time in what is now 11:35
Java. He is erect-standing, somewhat bigger brained
than *Homo habilis* and much bigger brained than the
clumsy australopithecines, who have by now ventured
out of Africa and with whom he shares the scene.
Finally the new man, *Homo erectus,* replaces the southern apes entirely. The new man and his sort hunt bigger
game, make better tools, are acquainted with the use of
fire. He becomes a traveler in the Old World.

Representatives of the *erectus* family have taken up
residence in Europe, Asia, the East Indies, and Africa.
Shown here are Java Man, China Man, and Chellean
Man from Africa.

11:45

The earliest representatives of *Homo sapiens*—Man the Wise—have appeared in what are now Germany and England (Swanscombe Man, shown here with light hair and beard). They are a bit thick of bone but much advanced in brain size over *Homo erectus,* with whom they most likely shared the world even before the third Ice Age began.

11:50

Later members of this newest group of men now begin to turn up in all continents of the Old World: Rhodesian Man in Africa (near the point where the clock hands meet); and in Europe, close to the last glacier, Neanderthal Man with his crooked legs, his prowlike nose, his flattened head (but very large brain). *Homo sapiens neanderthalensis* is his scientific name.

11:58

Homo sapiens sapiens—truly modern man, recent man—appears and stakes his claim.

Only modern man remains—alone of the *sapiens* types, alone of all the human players. Only he remains to people the earth. Over the Bering Strait he goes in the first invasion of the New World. His descendants there are to be the American Indians.

In the next half-minute he learns to herd the animals he formerly hunted and to grow food in the fruitful earth. With farming he settles down in villages and turns his hand and mind to still newer inventions.

The last twelve seconds of this Hour of Man represent all of recorded history. In these twelve seconds, we sail the seas, invent the wheel, learn to write, build cities, make laws, harness power, split the atom. We look backward at the road we have traveled and forward at the road that lies ahead.

In the whole of earth time these twelve seconds would hardly register a tick. Even the entire million and a half years of man's time add only a slightly longer tock. And yet, in our brief tick-tock we have tried much, suffered much, learned much.

Now we are preparing to leave our ancient home and explore the stars. Into a new and greater mystery we go—living creatures with the bodies of mammals, the hands and eyes of primates. We take with us wherever we go the long history of earth and the hopes, the dreams, of all the men before us, *all* the men of our little, little time.

PART TWO
BEING HUMAN

7

TOOLS, WEAPONS, FIRE
Mind Against Environment

Man has been called "the animal that laughs" as well as "the animal that cries." Scholars have dubbed him "Man the Playful" or "Man the Wise." But tears and laughter and wisdom leave no permanent witness behind. Only stones and sometimes bones outlast time and the processes of decay and erosion to tell us fragmentary stories of once living beings and the landscapes they inhabited. And it is when we find bones of creatures suspiciously like ourselves and, with those bones, ready to hand, pebbles which have been purposefully shaped and sharpened that we know we are confronting our own human ancestors—or if not our direct ancestors, then at least something very like them. So no matter how many other things man may have been all

at once—most certainly *was* all at once in his beginnings—we can know him first of all only as "Man the
Toolmaker."

A bit of sharpened stone may not seem to be a very
big beginning. "After all," you will say at once, "animals use tools too." And of course they do. Sea otters,
floating on their backs in the brine, crack clams between two stones laid on their broad chests. You have
certainly seen apes in captivity use boxes and sticks in
all sorts of clever ways to get at bananas just out of
reach. Not long ago, chimpanzees living in their native
Tanganyika forests were seen to probe termite hills
with twigs, fishing out the tasty larvae hidden in tun-
nels beneath the hard surface. What was really novel
was that the chimpanzees prepared their twigs before-
hand, plucking them off trees, stripping them of leaves,
and then carrying them long distances to the termite
hills. Though nothing like true toolmaking, this ability
to prepare, to modify, an implement is surely the next
best thing.

It is from just such an animal background of ever growing awareness and ingenuity that man's own intelligent brain emerged. Certainly it was not a very big brain when man first began to be human. The oldest skulls found in conjunction with made tools are scarcely larger than those of present-day anthropoid apes. But the tools prove that the brains behind them were already being used in an oddly different way, unique, really, in the animal world.

"How different?" you will want to know. And the best answer to this is a do-it-yourself one. Try being, for a little while, your own ancestor—a primitive creature with a pressing need for a sharp tool and only a rounded rock in hand. Try chipping out a cutting edge from that rock. You will soon discover it's no easy task. Unless you are aware of natural flaws, the rock fractures in odd places under your pounding. You will have to stop, patiently examine your stone core, and decide what its possibilities are. In your mind a picture will begin to form of the finished tool. That is the whole secret of the stone, of the implement in the stone, and of being human. The picture and the skill to recreate the picture—this is what sets man apart. This is the beginning of human culture. And now, enormously enlarged, enormously complex and enriched, the process of dream and picture and symbol has become man's whole life.

Besides testifying to man's ability to symbolize, purposely shaped pebble tools tell us that early man had

begun to understand the meaning of time—of past and future, instead of merely the present. They indicate that he was beginning, in a conscious way, to apply to future needs what he had learned from his past experience.

Pebble tools tell us that he was perhaps learning to make up for what he lacked in physical equipment. If you look at the jaws of the higher primates (our own jaws excepted), you will find them well provided with large, pointed, dangerous canine teeth—those fangs at the four corners of the mouth. Canines are useful in a fight and equally useful in eating tough foods, such as fruits with hard rinds or meat covered with thick hide. Most primates are not notable meat eaters—in spite of their formidable teeth. Of course, they are not above an occasional meal of small prey such as lizards and birds and rodents should they stray within reach. Baboon troops, in fact, are said to kill young lambs, and the Tanganyika chimpanzees have been seen to stalk and kill prey as large as young bushbucks. But these are exceptions. Most primates are by preference vegetarian.

Oddly enough, it was the beginning human creature with his insignificant set of chompers who became a meat eater and a hunter of meat. Perhaps he was deprived of his normal food supply and took to eating meat in order to survive. In any case, it is fairly certain that his diet was changed in spite of, not with the help of, his teeth, which were (like ours) incapable even of skinning a rabbit. (Several modern researchers have

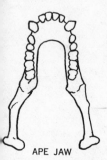

APE JAW

HUMAN JAW

tried in vain to do just that in order to prove the point!)
It was only with an extra "tooth" of stone that early
human creatures could skin and butcher their prey.

Some scientists believe that ancestors of the human
kind once really did have long canine teeth which grew
smaller when they were no longer needed for fighting
and defense, erect-standing near-men having learned to
use hand weapons instead. This may indeed be true.
All we know for sure is that no fossil primate—recognizably human through its association with stone tools
—has yet been found with teeth very different from our
own.

Sharpened stones, however, were probably not man's
first tools—certainly not his first weapons. Apes often
take a stick to their enemies or throw fruit or pebbles
or debris at them from the safety of the trees. And it is
reasonable to suppose that small and helpless beginning
man did these things too. Eventually, perhaps, he came
to realize how much protection a stick could be, and he
kept one around permanently. Maybe he found a stick
that just suited his hand, that was weighted just right,
that became polished from the oils of his skin. Maybe
he even gave the stick a name. It was *his*.

He must soon have discovered that with a pointed
end it was also useful for digging out the roots he liked
or for ripping open rotted logs so as to get at the tasty
grubs inside. Perhaps he learned to sharpen his stick by
rubbing it against rocky outcroppings or naturally
sharp stones. In time he must have tried sharpening

stones especially for this purpose, banging them against ledges to make the chips fly. In bad times, in dry times when vegetable foods became scarce, perhaps he was driven to hunting other animals—slow game such as tortoises or the young of large beasts or even his own kind. It was then he must have found that the sharpened stones had other uses beyond the pointing of sticks. It was then that stones became the fangs and claws he did not have and could not grow.

CHOPPER TOOL USED
BY HOMO ERECTUS

The known use of the stone "tooth" goes back a long, long way. When scientists first began to explore our past, it was thought that Neanderthal Man was the oldest, the most nearly beastlike, and the first toolmaker. We now know, of course, that he lived in comparatively recent times—no further distant than 50,000 years or so—that his brain was probably bigger than our own, and that he possessed a tool kit of great sophistication. He may have been the first man, for instance, to haft his weapons, to put the cutting stone point and the ever-useful wooden shaft together.

Homo erectus, though he lived 500,000 years ago, made stone tools of various kinds and for various uses —choppers and cleavers and axes of careful workmanship. Tools were being made nearly two million years ago. Pebbles, simply shaped and sharpened, have been found near the remains of *Zinjanthropus* and his clever neighbor, *Homo habilis.*

PEBBLE TOOL FOUND
NEAR ZINJANTHROPUS

From the earliest of the shaped stone tools to those of the time just before man discovered how to use metals, a slow progress can be seen, first in usefulness and then in beauty. At the very last, especially fine stone implements seem to have been used in religious ceremonies or as objects of reverence and respect.

We can follow the progress from the familiar pebble tool with a few flakes lopped off for sharpness to the fist ax. By this time men were more carefully choosing the stone core and then shaping it all over with a hammer stone for symmetry, edge, and balance. With the introduction of wooden strikers at a still later time, finer, more delicate shaping became possible, and men began producing beautiful implements. One of the hallmarks of this particular technique (called "Acheulian" after the place where tools of this type were first found) is the *S* shape you find on turning such a tool sidewise.

FIST AX

All through those long years (the Paleolithic, or Old Stone Age), men were of two schools of thought regarding their stone implements. The fist-ax makers—mostly dwellers in warm climes—were principally interested in the heavy stone core itself, which they trimmed to a desired form and used as an all-purpose tool. The waste flakes which flew off hither and yon were ground under foot and forgotten. People who lived nearer the glacial cold, however, apparently conceived the idea of using the flakes themselves. Perhaps these were especially useful in scraping and trimming animal skins to be used as protective clothing. The Neanderthals, as we have noted, delicately retouched flakes to make points which could have been hafted to spear shafts.

Other groups used a technique by which the core

ACHEULIAN FIST AX
(front and side views)

stone was carefully prepared to look much like a turtle with its head inside the shell. Then, a perfect blow on the shell top removed a blade ready for use without retouching.

Toward the end of the Paleolithic, some groups learned to turn out whole sets of knife blades from a core prepared with level striking platforms top and bottom. Retouched in various ways, they served any number of useful functions. A still newer technique permitted the manufacture of finer and smaller points. This was pressure flaking, by which the craftsman carefully *pried* off tiny flakes instead of striking them away with blows. Indian arrowheads—familiar to everyone —were made by this method.

By the time this system of manufacture had come into use, all species of men but our own had vanished. Gone were East African Man and all his southern cousins; gone Upright Man and all of his. Gone was Neanderthal Man—vanquished by us, succeeded by us, or perhaps merged into our own breed. The weaponry and the craftsmanship of all those men before us became part of our own tradition.

In the Middle and New Stone Ages we made tiny tools—microliths for saw teeth or bird arrows—and weapon heads of polished stone. We made bone and ivory tools—fish-hooks and blade handles and weapon straighteners and bows. The very tools we use today look much as they did in those early times, proving that the designs were good and lasting—or that we our-

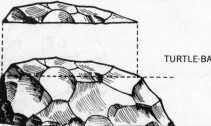

TURTLE-BACK CORE AND BLADE

selves change in some ways more slowly than we suppose.

When we speak of tools, we must not forget that fire, too, can be a tool and a weapon. Alone among animals, man uses it without fear and does not flee from its heat and light. In fire, wooden weapons can be hardened, straightened, and sharpened. With fire, trees can be felled and hollowed out for boats. Wooden blocks can be transformed into bowls. Fire protects and fire warms and fire draws the family together, pushing away the terrible dark with its animal predators and its nameless dread.

Meat can be eaten raw, of course, though cooking makes the eating of it go faster. But fire is absolutely essential in making certain important vegetable foods edible—grains, for example, or roots such as the poisonous manioc, so good and filling when its danger has been cooked away. Without fire, pottery might never have been invented or the use of metals learned. Without fire, man might have been forever a prisoner of the warmer parts of the world.

The discovery of fire's possibilities probably occurred some time after man's invention of tools. Fire, after all, is not the immediate necessity in warm climates that it is when the weather grows cold. And so it may not have been until beginning man moved slowly out of Africa and northward that he was driven to use fire. It is in caves in northern China, caves which were once inhabited by Upright Men, that we find the

first undoubted evidences of fire. Within the next 200,-
000 years, the use of fire spread to men everywhere, in
hot climates as well as cold.

Whether the men who *first* used it knew how to make
fire from the friction of rubbed wood or from the sparks
of struck flint we do not know. Perhaps they could only
gather the fire kindled when lightning struck a dead
tree or when a distant volcano sent burning cinders flying. Having brought such heaven-sent gifts home on
torches or in fire-pots, they must have fed the fire carefully as one feeds a precious and hungry animal, keeping its flames alive at all costs.

In such remote experiences we can see the dim out-
lines of the Prometheus story, so often retold in the
myths of all peoples everywhere. From such distant beginnings, we can understand why fire was honored and
worshipped and tended; why the chief altars of many
folk were their family hearths; and why the graves of
our own honored dead are still marked by an eternal
flame.

THE HUMAN FAMILY
Adding Father

Monkeys and apes are social animals. They live in groups with varying numbers of individuals—from the orangutan's three or four to the baboon troop's hundred or so. The size of the different groups seems to be related partly to the environment, partly to the available food, partly to particular eating habits. Whether the individual animals are large or small, whether they live mostly on the ground or mostly in the trees, and whether they are peaceable or rowdy also seem to make a difference.

Man, too, is a social being and certainly must have been so in his beginnings. But his group life has come to be less and less determined by the actual physical environment and more and more related to his ways of

behaving. Learned ways of behaving, unlike biologi-
cally given ones, can vary infinitely. A human being
from any sort of background can learn to live in any
other environment. If he comes to the "different"
society at an early age, he will have no difficulty whatever in adjusting. For social behavior is not part of
man in the same way that his hair or skin color or
length of leg are part of him. Ways of behaving socially
may often seem instinctive; they are really only habits,
and habits can be unlearned and replaced by ones better suited to a given situation. This is not to say that
animals do not learn, but they are not the thorough-
going students of experience that man came to be.
Surely it was this ability to learn that gave us our biggest boost in leaving behind the world of our animal
cousins.

Just when and how the shift-over happened—from
societies based partly on learning, partly on instinct, to
societies built almost totally on learned tradition—we
do not know. Unlike tools, changes in behavior leave
no marks behind. Educated guesses can be made, however. An anthropologist takes what is known about the
simplest living hunting people and projects backward.
Then he considers what has been learned from observing apes and monkeys in their native homes and thinks
forward. Somewhere between the two kinds of behavior
he can imagine patterns that might have been true for
early man.

We would not be too far wrong in looking first for

changes in the primate family unit. Now, except for the gibbon and the tiny marmoset, most primates do not sort themselves into families as we think of them. Generally, they move about in groups led by one or several dominant males who are fathers of all the group young. The word "fathers," in this sense, does not imply that they take any responsibility in caring for or feeding the assorted infants, though they may be affectionate enough in an offhand way. But they do act to protect the entire group of females and young. The real *family* unit among primates consists only of a mother and one or two offspring, for bringing up a baby is the mother's job entirely. By and large, as among most mammals, the primate mom does a good job of it. And there is much to do. Aside from the business of feeding and tending and guarding from harm, primate mothers must teach their babies a goodly number of things, such as how to weave a nest for the night, how to dig for roots and grubs, and how to behave around older members of the group. There is even good evidence that, without a mother to teach her, a primate daughter cannot herself become a good mother.

Primate mothers can handle all these responsibilities

MOTHER GORILLA AND BABY

alone well enough so long as food is easily come by. But man, you will remember, quite early in his career ceased to be a gatherer and became a hunter. Now, female creatures, burdened with infants and half-grown children, can hunt very little. And when infants are as helpless at birth and helpless for as long as the human baby, mothers are entirely dependent on males to provide the food. This kind of thoughtfulness, however, is not ordinarily normal to the primate male. In sight of food it's usually every ape for himself and ladies to the end of the line.

To find a model for our human father-provider we shall have to look elsewhere in the animal world. Hunting animals, rather than primate vegetarians, would seem to offer the better choice. Wolves, for example, often mate for life, raise their cubs together, and together, teach them to hunt. The father wolf feeds the mother when she is nursing and helps supply the cubs with meat once they are weaned.

It must have been by slow degrees that the beginning human family added such a father. We can get just a hint of how the change might have come about by turning once again to those unusual meat-eating chimpanzees observed in the Tanganyika wild by a British zoologist, Miss Jane Goodall. She once saw a large male gallantly stand aside from his freshly killed dinner to allow a female holding a tiny baby to eat her fill. None of the male onlookers was permitted so much as a taste though they all begged and begged.

Perhaps early human hunters similarly allowed females to share in their kills. An occasional meat dinner could always be eked out with fruits and leaves, which the females could get for themselves. But when meat became the all-important item of diet—perhaps also when vegetation became scarce—the hunter must have found his work overwhelming. Eventually, perhaps, each male in a band concentrated on feeding just one female (at most, two) and their joint offspring. And so began the integrated human family, a hunting family, with a father.

Adding Daddy to the family did more for developing human kind than just settling the dinner problem. The novelty of shared experiences caused both male and female to learn and grow and care for each other. Early man, who had already become brighter by way of toolmaking, introduced woman to the use and need of "kitchen implements." And woman, who had long been growing brighter just through having to cope with babies, handed Junior over to Daddy now and then, to the general improvement of both. Human babies by that time really needed the extra care, for they were maturing much more slowly than their primate cousins. The longer dependent childhood gave their heads and brains a chance to grow. It provided a longer period in which learning could take place. It also held the family together longer, making fast the bonds of affection and need.

By and by, as man had to range with his fellows

farther and farther afield in search of game, other things happened. Woman became the keeper of the home, the gatherer of supplementary vegetable foods. Confined to home base, however, she must have developed a powerful curiosity about what went on in the all-male hunting world. As the American zoologist William Etkin suggests, this curiosity may even have helped to push along the invention of language. One of the first sentences uttered must surely have been a variation on the classic "What happened today at the office, dear?"

Children began to remain with their parents longer and longer, sometimes even after growing up. They chose—or stole—mates from other family groups and brought them home to Papa and Mama. The boys and young men helped in the hunting. The girls helped around the camp and sat with one another's babies. Perhaps they were joined in time by other family groups. Not too many, however, for hunting bands must remain small lest excess numbers deplete the game.

With the expansion of the group and the widening of mental horizons, definite rules had to be made—rules to keep the group happy or, at least, willing to put up with one another. Hunters had to know which man would get which parts of the animals cooperatively slain. They had to know what sort of behavior was expected of them during the hunt. And they had to know that the women and girls left behind in the camp were

following the rules set out for *them,* for hunters cannot
work well if they have to worry about what is going on
at home. Eventually there had to be rules about how
the young people were to marry. Because no family
wanted to be deprived of a grown son's or daughter's
help, rules of exchange developed. "You give us a
daughter for our son," one man would say to his friend,
"and we'll give you a daughter for *your* son."

Marriage with outsiders brought more and more
people within the circle of family care and concern.
And it was now a very conscious care and concern.
People and relationships were no longer easily forgotten—even after death. Not, at least, in the old primate
way: out of sight, out of mind!

As families grew and more and more relatives were

acknowledged, additional rules appeared. They were meant to insure cooperation and help in times of trouble, meant to give people a sense of belonging and support in a world becoming ever more frightening as man's growing consciousness made him an alien in it. Still other rules determined whether young people would take their names from their mother's or from their father's family and to which group they would belong the more. If their main membership was in the father's group, then Father and his brothers would have the greatest say in their upbringing. The boys would inherit their father's hunting weapons and his songs and his magic. If, on the other hand, they were considered primarily members of their mother's group, then her brothers had the most say and it was from them that the boys received their inheritance. Father then became only a pleasant companion—the person you told your troubles to.

Though this sort of arrangement does seem to emphasize one side of the family at the expense of the other, no one was ever really left out of a child's life. All relatives played important roles, though not always the same ones in every group of people. If Father's family gave names and property, then Mother's relatives usually gave the child warmer affection. They were the ones who petted and "spoiled" him, with never a spank or a scolding word. If Mother's brothers gave name and goods, why, just the reverse; it was then Father's relatives who were the loving ones.

In time and with prosperity, different kinds of marriages came into vogue. Some groups thought a man should have many wives—as many as he could comfortably support or as he needed to support him. Some groups thought a woman should have several husbands. Some confined themselves to one spouse each way. This marriage form, which is called monogamy, is followed by the simplest of present-day hunting people, on the one hand, and the most sophisticated of city dwellers, on the other.

Many of these systems of marriage and reckoning of relatives had then and have now very little bearing, really, on the elementary needs of life. They have instead to do with something that is peculiarly human: a sense of fitness and propriety, right and wrong, of what has worth and what does not. No two groups of people have just the *same* notions of worth. Certainly such notions grow and change. But all human beings have values. People strive to live up to their group's ideals— whether those ideals turn on a certain kind of marriage or on proper behavior or on loyalty to a particular set of relatives. Indeed, they must conform in order to remain part of the group.

If notions of worth help keep a people together, they can cause divisions too. For notions of worth apply not just to groups of people but to individuals within each group. Every human being longs to be important, to be noticed, to be admired, to be valued. And some are willing to fight to achieve distinction. We can see a

reflection of this urge in the animal world, most often among males who battle each other, for mates, sometimes for food, occasionally just to see which is strongest. When we get to the primates, something very like the learning process enters the picture. A monkey's position in his band, his rank, for instance, is sometimes determined as much by his mother's closeness to the old leader as by his own strength and cunning. The old saying, "Them that has, *gits!*" apparently has a great deal more than simply human application.

In man, the longing for superiority becomes still more complex. For he has, inside his head, pictures of himself as he wants to be, as he thinks he *ought* to be. The pictures are conditioned, first of all, by what his group considers of greatest worth—whether it is the family into which one is born, one's own skills as a hunter or dancer or medicine man, or perhaps one's wealth or property. The pictures grow as a man compares himself with other men. Most often they can be realized only as he struggles to be better, somehow, than the man next door—worthier, more human, even more divine. In this kind of rivalry, group traditions of worth change little by little, perhaps bearing down harder on particular values, perhaps shifting to other ideas entirely.

Being superior always seems to matter to some people more than to others. In very simple societies, individual excellence is deeply distrusted, for it causes resentment and disrupts the group. In such societies, it is thought far safer for everyone to be as much as possible like everyone else. Individuals who push just a little too hard, who are just a little more ambitious than the others are punished in one way or another. Sometimes they are even accused of acquiring their superior talents by evil witchcraft and are driven from the group. Often such groups cannot even tolerate leaders above the heads of individual families. When leaders do emerge, they are often so burdened with responsibilities as to make their added importance hardly worth the candle. Thus is individual competitiveness balanced out by the urgent need for group cooperation and solidarity.

When human societies began to grow larger and more complex, when men no longer had to worry every minute about the next meal, there came to be a great many different ways of achieving worth. People could be recognized as good artists or good businessmen or good scholars. Hunter and warrior were no longer the only roles a man could play. And women began eventually to share in the new pursuits, achieving importance in fields other than motherhood. With the new roles of importance, which allowed more people to feel appreciated in more and more ways, societies grew and were enriched.

In larger societies state governments began to replace the family as the source of rules. First chiefs, then kings, then whole networks of officials—elected or appointed—replaced family heads as leaders. And written laws replaced traditional rules as the basis of group behavior. Without the restraining web of kinship, with mass communication and mass control, individual struggles for power and position could take place on a higher, more dangerous plane. Even so, however, the drives of the competitive few were (and are still) checked by the needs of the many. A responsible leader of any time—from the earliest of chiefs to the latest of prime ministers—has always had to take those many into account lest his own unrestricted desire for worth make him less human than he really meant to be.

9

LANGUAGE
The Magic of Symbol

"In the beginning," writes St. John, "was the word." Certainly it was with the word that man found his own proper role on the stage of creation. Words became his tools as much as any fist ax. Like clubs and cleavers, words enabled him to control his environment—but to control it in a mental way. No longer was he to be acted upon by an indifferent nature, for with words he discovered the power of will, the power of magic.

It was not quite the kind of magic he at first imagined it to be. He could not summon game animals by calling on their "real names," though such was his belief. He could not quiet a storm or harness the lightning in a net of words. But naming the things around him gave man power over them, all the same. For to name a creature is, in a way, to master it. To name a

139

fear is to lessen its terror. To name a thing unknown is already to begin to understand its meaning.

The power of words must have been a very early gift. Surely it appeared not long after man had begun to fashion tools shaped to a special pattern. A tool and a word are really much alike in one very important way. Though one is a thing—you can see it and touch it— and the other is a sound, they are both the outward expressions of ideas. They are *symbols* of ideas. The brain that can picture the way a tool should look and then direct the hands to copy that picture is certainly capable of giving the picture a name. And just as there was a feedback from hand to brain—the greater the manual skill, the better the brain behind it—so, too, was there a feedback from word to brain. We think largely by means of words or of some other symbols. (Musicians, no doubt, think in musical notes when they are composing, and mathematicians solve problems with the symbolic shorthand of their calling.) The greater the number of words we possess, the sharper, the more perceptive are our thoughts.

Another reason why words must have accompanied toolmaking was the very real problem of passing on the manufacturing secrets. A man, after all, wants to share new knowledge with his children, to give them whatever edge he can in the struggle for survival. And this must have been as true in those early times as it is today. Now, if you have ever worked at flaking a lump of quartz or flint, you know how difficult it is to keep the chips from falling where they may. You are far likelier to cut your fingers than you are to achieve an edge that will cut anything else. But only let an expert tell you *in words* at what angle you must strike the core, how much force to exert, and what to use as a hammer, and you soon learn to produce a good pebble tool. The fact that hand axes the world over are remarkably similar in pattern proves that somebody was teaching somebody else, and undoubtedly words carried the bulk of the information.

We must not suppose, however, that because we communicate ideas and instruct by means of words this is their only function. We use words to express our feelings, too, just as animals use grunts or barks or squeals. We might say "I hate you!" to another person instead of growling and baring our fangs. We cry "Look out!" when we want to warn someone of danger. We call "Help!" when we are in trouble. We use words to be friendly, too, to show that we are pleasant, sympathetic, and certainly not a threat to anyone.

Professor Etkin thinks the use of words in promoting friendly feelings may have been at least partly responsible for the loss of our body hair. Have you ever noticed how much time zoo primates spend grooming each other? With unflagging patience they comb through the

MONKEYS GROOMING

hair of offspring or friend, searching out lice or bits of
dirt lodging therein. Then the roles are reversed in this
"you-scratch-my-back-I'll-scratch-yours" game, the fa-
vorite occupation of primates in the wild as well as of
primates in captivity. For grooming provides something more than just mutual cleaning and some in-
cidental insect delicacies. It is a prime means of social-
izing, of relating one ape to another. When man found
words he used them instead to promote friendly feelings. If you listen sometime to the chatter at any party,
you will see this is so. The flow of information has
slowed to a trickle, but the flow of friendliness engulfs
all in waves of meaningless words. It is verbal grooming.

We have the animal world to thank for our ability to
communicate on any level—informative, emotional, or
social (with or without grooming). For all living creatures manage some form of communication. The dance
patterns of bees in their hive help to point the way to
distant flower fields or announce successful foraging.
Male stickleback fish regularly swim upside-down to
indicate outrage in a courtship contest. Male deer and
lemurs mark territorial ownership by rubbing their own
body secretions on boundary stones or trees. Everyone
has seen a frightened dog put his tail between his legs
and run in panic. We, too, use gestures, expressions,
postures, and movement to give our words point.

But, by and large, the higher one climbs up the
family tree, the more one encounters the predominant

use of vocal patterns in communication. Birds sing, and some of them can be taught to imitate the human voice —though not, of course, to understand what the words mean. Cats and dogs snarl and bark, and yowl. Horses whinny, camels gurgle, hyenas "laugh." The clever dolphin is said to have an impressive range of sounds which, sonar-like, he transmits through water.

Observers of our own primate relatives in their native habitats report plenty of vocalizing here, too. Gorillas and orangs tend to be strong, silent types, but chimpanzees, gibbons, and some of the monkeys can be vocal about specific situations in more than twenty separate sounds. These noises, however, are not words, not a language—although we can think of them as the rough matrix in which our own gift of language was formed. They are simply signals meant to summon or frighten or warn. They cannot convey abstract information. A chimpanzee's grunt of suspicion might very well succeed in sending his band scampering up a tree and out of harm's way. But it could not possibly tell them that the approaching (and possibly dangerous) stranger walks upright on two legs, is relatively hairless, and holds something in his hand that may or may not be a weapon.

It is at this point of communicating abstract information that we leave our nearest animal kin behind. Even with the most devoted care and instruction, the clever chimpanzee cannot be taught to imitate more than one or two human words, and even then it is not

certain whether he can fully make the connection between the word and the thing it represents. Whether the
lack of full-time upright posture has restricted his vocal
equipment, or whether his brain is simply not geared to
handle complex symbols, the fact remains that language is (as far as we now know) a uniquely human
achievement.

It used to be a popular game among scholars fifty or
so years ago to make learned guesses about the origin
of words and why they had taken just the forms they
did. There had to be, some theorists held, a mystic connection between every word and its meaning. Others
thought words developed from ejaculations of surprise
or even from work chants. Still others saw words as
imitations of natural sounds—the barking of dogs,
gurgle of water, whisper of wind. (Linguist M. Pei
terms these notions the Ding-Dong, Pooh-Pooh, Yo-
He-Ho, and Bow-Wow theories.) The trouble with
such theories was that no two languages seem to have
exclaimed alike or grunted alike or even imitated the
same natural sounds in quite the same way. Roosters in
America crow with a "cock-a-doodle-do." Italian listen-
ers translate the same sound into "chichirichi," while
Frenchmen hear it as "cocorico." Mystic connections
cannot account for word forms. As Shakespeare wrote,
"a rose by any other name would smell as sweet."

Scholars who turned to the languages of so-called
primitives, seeking from them the key to man's ancestral speech, were likewise disappointed. The truth

is that there are no primitive languages spoken on this earth. No matter how simple the culture, you will not find its people limited to a basic word list like "Me Tarzan, you Jane." Among every people the language spoken is perfectly adequate for the way of life. Often, indeed, the languages of the simplest peoples are the most formidably complex. The Australian Aborigines, surely among the world's poorest in terms of material culture, are extraordinarily rich in kinship titles. They would think us very backward with our one word for "cousin," which has to make do for relatives on both sides of the family and in all degrees. Polynesians use an extensive vocabulary of sailing terms and words to describe the sea in its many aspects. Each kind of wave —whether high or low, peaceful or dangerous—has its own specific name. To the Eskimos, snow in all its various consistencies requires the same careful labeling.

All peoples tend to give verbal stress to those things in their lives they find most important. Each looks at life a little differently; each classifies objects and ideas in a slightly differing order, with a slightly varying emphasis. In this respect, language is a kind of science as well as magic.

If you speak French or Spanish you know that all nouns in those languages come equipped with gender. An apple is not just an apple, unspecified and of itself; it is *la pomme,* a female apple. Pencil, by the same token, becomes *le crayon,* with a gentlemanly article attached. In other languages, nouns are described as

AUSTRALIAN ABORIGINE
WITH HIS DOG

being living or inanimate in addition to possessing gender. Still others classify in terms of size, shape, and constitution—whether animal, vegetable, or mineral.

The Bantu languages provide for these terms of description by tacking on to each noun an identifying prefix. The prefix for personal beings is *mu* in the singular, *ba* in the plural. When discussing another group of people—the Mbuti group of Pygmies, for example—a Bantu speaker would call them the Ba-Mbuti —people first and Pygmies after. In Bantu, classification calls for judgment and fine distinctions, and the prefix chosen had better be the right one, because it will color nearly every other word in the sentence. The language student might well dither a bit over a word like *knife*. Should it have the "long, pointed" prefix or the one meaning "instrument"?

Words are not all there is to language, however. They must be strung together in some kind of statement to make sense. Every statement, or sentence, in every language usually describes some kind of action being performed by someone or something. Often another person or thing acted upon is involved. "Dog bites man." That is about as bare and simple as a basic statement can be. Some languages, such as Latin, however, want to make doubly clear who is doing what to whom, so they add to the subject and object special endings which tell precisely what they are. They could then be all mixed up in the sentence; the meaning would still be clear. In English, on the other hand, one must be careful of placement, or else one gets "Man bites dog"—surely a very different story.

Besides the bare-bones statements common to all languages, many relational forms are used to enhance the meaning. We usually start by saying "*the* man" and "*the* dog," and, if we want to be extra specific, "*that* man." Maybe the dog didn't confine his attentions to one man. Here we add a number concept, and "man" becomes plural. "The dog bites several *men*." If the action happened yesterday, then the dog "*bit*"—in the past tense. And, by the way, whose dog was it? (to add a fillip of the possessive). We might further describe both man and dog in terms of color, age, size, and temper.

The ways in which all these modifications are worked into the basic statement differ markedly from language to language. In English—and even more so in Chinese, which is as innocent of grammar as a telegram—all these concepts would, by and large, be expressed in separate words: "My black male dog bit the angry men yesterday."

In other languages, again using Latin as an example, many of the auxiliary concepts (time, number, gender) might be worked into the basic statement in such a way that each word does double, even triple, duty. *Ille ater canis homines iratos mordebatur,* which simply means "the black dog bit the angry men," can be literally translated thus: "*that*-one-masculine-doer, one-*black*-masculine-doer, masculine-doing-one-*dog,* being-done-to-masculine-plural-*men,* being-done-to-masculine-plural-*angry,* third-person-one (not you or I but he, the dog)-then (not now)-*bit.*"

Other languages—those of the American Indians, for instance—go all the way in this direction. The auxiliary ideas and even the subject and object attach themselves to the verb in such a way as to form a one-word sentence. Here is an example: *inialudam.* In the Chinook tongue of the American Northwest Coast, this means "I came to give it to her." The basic element is *-d-,* "to give." All the other concepts hang on so tightly as to form a single unified word-sentence. Languages using this kind of fusing for basic statement and related concepts are called "polysynthetic" (many-merging).

Besides these different degrees of combination, languages can be further classified by the way in which the concepts merge. When a number of individual words are run together in such a fashion as to form one big word but with all the parts still able to go their separate ways, this is called "agglutination"—roughly, a sort of glueing process. In our own language this process can be seen in words like *beautiful.* It was originally *full of beauty. Coffee break* and *home run,* after a period of hyphenation, will probably one day be glued into *coffeebreak* and *homerun,* single words whose parts still retain their individual identities.

In other languages, however, the parts lose their

identities and cannot be unstuck. The parts are less glued than welded. This process is called "inflection." In it, words consist of fragmentary stems or roots carrying the basic meaning and of auxiliary concepts tacked on fore and aft. Latin is an inflected language. So are the Semitic tongues such as Hebrew and Arabic. These prefer stems consisting of three consonants. The changing vowels in the middle tell time, number, possession, etc. The group *k-t-b* conveys the idea of writing. As *kataba* it means "he has written"; as *katib,* "writer"; as *kitab,* "book." This reminds us of English words like *to sing,* which, with internal vowel changes, becomes *sang* and then *sung.*

Languages which have similar structural patterns and many similar words can sometimes be found to be related, to belong in the same "family." Astute detective work can even determine the degree of relationship —whether sister, cousin, or kissing kin. Often the ancestral language, long gone and forgotten, can be reconstructed from the patterns of its descendants. Whole movements of peoples can be traced across continents by the casual deposits of words they left behind. The degree of difference between related languages can often tell the scholar how long the people who speak those languages have been separated and where they came from originally. So words are history, too.

History can be read in the way words change. For, like everything else in life, words do change. Even their patterning in language changes. English, for example, in its Anglo Saxon youth was highly inflected like all its other language relatives. In the course of time, it became simplified, streamlined, pared down. Now, although family resemblances can still be read in its words, its basic structure has tended to become more like Chinese than anything else.

Why do languages change? Perhaps we could better ask how. People are highly susceptible to outside influences, always on the lookout for something new, and this is reflected in language. Sometimes these new influences appear violently by way of war and conquest. Let us say one of our early groups of men overran another group. Instead of eating their victims, they might agree to a merger of tribes. But naturally they would insist on *their* names for gods and fist axes being used.

NEANDERTHALER WITH
HAFTED SPEAR

Diffusion is a gentler way of introducing new ideas and the words that go with them. Picture our friend Neanderthal Man (he who was first, you will remember, to haft his weapons) admiring a newly made spear. He stands on a rocky ledge in the bright, chilly sunshine, very pleased with himself and with the world. He doesn't know he is being watched by an enemy—one of those "new" men from across the gorge. The enemy admires the fine spear, too, grasping instantly the possibilities of its use. Maybe he is even close enough to hear the name our Neanderthaler gives it. Too intrigued to think of snatching the weapon from its owner, or maybe too unsure of the terrain to risk a fight, the "new" man rushes home to duplicate what he has seen. And when he finishes, he calls the weapon by the same name the Neanderthaler used—and so do his sisters and his cousins and his aunts—and the tribe twenty miles up the glacier who steal the idea from *him*.

Drift accounts for language changes, too. Hunting bands can seldom number more than a few individuals. The uncertain food supply prohibits a big population. When the group grows, in times of plenty, beyond a certain reasonable limit, its people have to split into separate bands and move away from each other. If they move far enough away, if natural barriers like mountains and lakes divide them permanently, and if enough time is allowed to elapse, their common language will first split into separate dialects, then gradually evolve into different tongues. There will always be the family

resemblances we have mentioned, but the pronuncia-
tion of words will change, just as new words will arise
to describe things and experiences which the parent
group cannot share. Often, old words will take on new
meanings or be used in connection with very different
customs adopted from people new to the migrating
group.

Because of all these changes, people who look alike
sometimes do not speak the same language. People who
have the same customs sometimes do not look alike.
Looks, language, and ways of living are not necessarily
bound together. No group speaks a preordained language meant for it alone. Neither is there a mystic connection between a thing and the vocal symbol which
represents it. A fist ax can be a *coup de poing,* or a
core biface so long as two or more people subscribe to
those terms: it is still a stone meant to cut.

Troubles with language arise when people forget
that words are only symbols, after all. They do not
have inherent meanings apart from those we attach to
them. And the meanings we attach somehow always
differ, ever so slightly, from one person to the next. For
if groups of people differ in personality and outlook,
individuals differ also within a general pattern. Because
our behavior is learned behavior, because we are not
guided and pushed by instinct alone, we can grow up
marked by differing individual experiences and with
different feelings about the words that describe them.
The child who, on his third birthday, trips and falls

headlong into the birthday cake, spoiling the feast and his new suit, is bound to have ever after slightly different feelings about the words *birthday cake* from those of the child who each year unfailingly and properly blows out all the candles.

Because of these slight differences in meaning, people—even in the same family—often fail to communicate properly; they misunderstand each other, they quarrel. When misunderstandings occur on an international level, all sorts of eruptions can ensue, eruptions which can threaten human beings everywhere.

The gift of language cuts both ways. Its magic has opened for us the wonderful world of dreams. But it can still unleash a nightmare.

10

CLOTHING AND SHELTER
Yes, But Is It Beautiful?

An American blonde with her hair over one eye or a Japanese actress with a traditional headdress might win admiring glances in any capital of the Western world. But among the Sara people of Africa neither would hold a candle to the local belle, lips distended by loops or disks of wood, head bent to the weight of her enormous "bill." The men of ancient Egypt, on the other hand, admired exaggerated almond eyes, heavy black wigs, and dog-collar necklaces. Ladies of fashion no doubt labored long at their paint pots to achieve the desired effect. "Beauty," goes the old saying, "is in the eye of the beholder." One might also add: "and in the standards of his own home town."

Actually the Sara custom of enormously enlarging a girl's lips with bigger and bigger disks of wood may

155

have been begun with practical ends in view, perhaps
when the Sara people (living along the Ubangi River in
jungle Africa) were being raided by slavers who carted
off all the women in sight. Somebody got the idea that
if the women were made ugly enough, nobody would
want them for slaves any more. The idea worked, apparently, but after a while people forgot about why the
custom had been started. The clapping lips had become
a great big beauty mark.

Many ideas of beauty begin, in fact, with an element
of need. In the animal world—even in the plant world
—need and beauty seem tightly bound. The brilliant
plumage of a male bird—which so charms both the human bird-watcher and the lady bird herself—really
serves to protect the baby birds still in their shells. The
drab little mother can sit inconspicuously on her nest
while the gaudy father distracts the hunter's eye.

The bright (or drab) plumages we wear today do a
lot more than simply cover (or sometimes not cover)
our nakedness. They announce a great many things
about us: how much money we have, how important
we are, how vain or clever or beauty-loving. Sometimes
they tell what jobs we do. Often they tell things we
would rather were kept secret. But, like the bird's
plumage, clothes answered once and answer still a very
real need. They were a very *conscious* invention. Once
man had lost his primate body hair, he could not grow
it again—no more than he could regrow fang or claw.
So, just as the wooden club and the stone tool became

man's artificial fang and claw, hides stolen from other animals became his artificial pelt.

He must have needed this pelt soon after he moved northward. If—as many scientists now believe—man's birthplace was in Africa, he would not have needed clothes there. The African climate seems always to have been warm even when the rest of the world was clothed in glacial ice. It was rainy during those times, but seldom cold. Why man moved is hard to guess. As a hunter, perhaps he gradually followed his animal quarry north. He may have made the journey during periods of warmth. Settled in the north, however, he found the climate soon enough becoming distinctly uncomfortable. Unfamiliar snow fell, water froze. He may have found fire at this time. But fire, like shelter, provides warmth only when you stay in one spot. It is no help when you have to be out and doing. For that you need portable warmth of some kind. Real cold cannot be survived without it.

Discovering clothing was probably not much of a trick. After all, animals had to be skinned to be eaten, and man had been doing a pretty good job of that for quite some time. The difficult thing was to prepare the skins so that they would not spoil and rot and fall apart. Stone tools of this time, especially those found in northern sites, began to be shaped for scraping the flesh off hides, getting as close to the skin as possible.

Primitive hunting people of today stretch hides in the air to dry, treat them with water and fatty substances mixed with animal brains and liver, chew them to keep them soft, and rub them with stones to make them smooth. Probably early man tried these methods of curing too.

At first he simply wore the hides slung over his back or hung around his waist. Even such a flapping garment can help keep out the cold. The Indians of Tierra del Fuego—at the frigid southern tip of South America—were still using such clothing and only such clothing in 1832 when they were encountered by Charles Darwin as he sailed around Cape Horn in the H.M.S. *Beagle*. The Indians draped their little guanaco-hide or sea-otter cloaks between themselves and the wind—from whichever direction it was blowing. And that was all the protection they had. It is true, of course, that, like

FUEGAN TRIBESMAN

the Eskimos up north, Fuegan Indians are physically better adapted to endure cold weather than the rest of us. Their stumpy, short limbs and heavy bodies, the whole well insulated with fat, can better conserve heat than tall, stringy bodies from whose extended skin surfaces heat is given off at a great rate. Bean-pole types are better adapted to life in the hot spots of this earth.

Whatever natural help the Fuegans had when they arrived in the New World, however, they could not have survived the rigors of Cape Horn without some artificial protection—fire, shelter, clothing. And these they had, though the clothing was only a cloak. They also smeared themselves liberally with animal fat with much the same motive that prompts endurance swimmers today to grease up before taking the plunge. The Fuegans often decorated their suits of lard with brightly colored clay arranged in artistic designs. Enter beauty on the scene—and a new meaning for what began merely as a means of protection.

The tool kits of men who lived soon after Neanderthal times included stone and bone instruments which we know as awls—punches, really. Similar tools are used by primitive hunters even today to make holes in skins. Through these, strips of hide or lengths of twisted sinew can be threaded to make real clothes—if not tailored, at least shaped to cover the body more completely than cloak or loin cloth.

The next step in the development of the early garment industry was the invention of the bone needle.

Our own kind of men—or women—made clothes sewn with bone needles which probably looked much like the wonderful, practical clothing Eskimos wear today: inner garments with fur turned to the skin; outer garments for added warmth. But the ladies did not stop there. Even a king's ransom in furs was not enough. They began embroidery. Intricate designs in porcupine quills began to appear on the skins and furs. Beauty again.

Later still when man became a farmer and herder and moved further around the world, he found different materials for his clothing. He began to cut the wool from his sheep instead of killing them for their hides. This wool he learned to spin (or rather, his wife did) into thread and then to weave it on looms into fabric. And he found the selfsame process worked also with plant fibers, such as those from flax and cotton, or insect fibers, such as those from the silk-worm cocoon. In the tropics he learned to beat the inner bark of the mulberry tree into paper material which he (and his wife) wore wrapped around themselves in the familiar sarong. On the northern plains he tried the beating method with wool, matting it into felt. And never, never was the simple material, the simple garment enough. He learned to color his materials as well, to print them with designs, to cut them, and to ornament them with pins, rings, and necklaces of stone or bone.

In time, special colors were reserved for special people, as purple has come to be associated with royalty. Special head gear indicated position and importance

ESKIMO WOMAN

and occupation. Special and costly materials were worn by people to show they could pay the cost. Sometimes the cut of the clothing, its heaviness or unwieldiness or particular discomfort showed that the wearer could afford to be thus encumbered and kept from doing useful work. Who would have expected to find a woman of Civil War times scrubbing the floor in a crinoline? Who would expect to see a modern girl hanging up wet clothes while wearing spike heels (except maybe in magazine ads)?

Garments have not provided the only means of announcing wealth or rank or job or state of mind. Such announcements regularly turned up in the hair or on the skin or in the flesh of man. For we are a species that, seemingly, can never leave ourselves alone. We must be forever improving on what nature gave us. We put bones in our noses, file our teeth, pierce our ears. We flatten youngsters' heads, elongate their necks, scarify their skins. In Manchu China, daughters of wealthy families had their feet tightly bound as babies so that they could never grow, never be walked on. Like high heels and hoop skirts, "lily feet" announced that a girl would never have to scrub floors, not if her family had anything to say about it.

And always there has been paint. The use of clay-colored fat among the Fuegans tells us how body painting might have begun—a by-product of the search for warmth. The utilitarian aspects have long since disappeared. Among simple people in warm climates paint is often a decoration, a mark of rank, an item of dress.

TIV WOMAN WITH
ORNAMENTAL SCARS

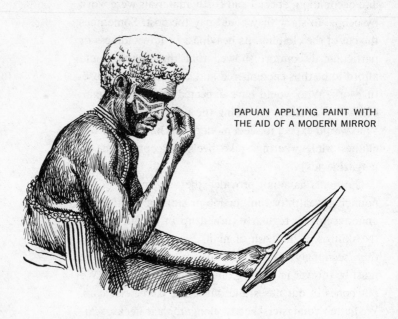

PAPUAN APPLYING PAINT WITH
THE AID OF A MODERN MIRROR

A man who might appear stark naked with perfect com-
posure would not be caught dead without his coat of
paint. We paint too, though among civilized societies
such display is usually confined to the human female.
Our male birds wear the dull plumage here. And what
selective advantages do you suppose there are to that?

Most living things are homebodies. To bees and
chipmunks and bower birds and bears there's no place

like home—meaning, respectively, hive or hole, bower or cave. Home for many animals means simply the nursery where babies are born and in which they are protected until they are able to face the world. Some others include a piece of real estate along with the house and carefully mark off the property by leaving their body secretions on trees and stones all along the boundary lines. (No trespassers, please!) The higher apes move from one tree to another, never calling any special one home. But, liking solid comfort, they regularly make sleeping nests each night and sometimes for afternoon naps as well. Not very many animals, except the hibernating ones, really need homes for shelter. But man does, and man did.

At first he must have followed the lead of his primate cousins, climbing trees at night, or maybe huddling in tight groups on the ground. Dr. Leakey, whose diggings at Olduvai revealed so many early human remains, has unearthed circular structures of piled-up stones suspiciously like windbreaks. These were found on the same level as (though not alongside) the earliest evidence of *Homo habilis,* whose age, you will recall, has been estimated at nearly 2 million years. Man may thus have become something of a builder far earlier than anyone has supposed. It is safe to say, however, that he did not take to permanent shelter until he moved north. He must have noticed that bears and certain other animals found sheltered lairs in natural caves, and being nothing if not a superb learner, decided to use the caves himself. Actually, there is considerable evidence that, in Europe at least, he really shared the caves with the giant cave bear. This is probably not so dangerous an undertaking as it might seem. The bear spends his winter in deep sleep, and his caves quite likely provided Neanderthal Man with the first stocked refrigerators in history.

It is a lucky thing for us our ancestors took to cave living. For it is in those caves that we find preserved for us to see some record of life in those times. For they were careless housekeepers. Careless? Messy is a better word. Tools, left-over dinners, bones, debris, and garbage were simply trod under foot and lived with. Even the dead were buried under the cave floor and thus kept near their living loved ones. All this was not really so unsanitary as it sounds. The cold weather of glacial times kept caves from being utterly unlivable even for creatures without a conditioned sense of smell. The men who followed Neanderthal were certainly no tidier. And, in addition to the usual litter underfoot, they fortunately left us wonderful paintings slapped helter-skelter over the walls of some of their caves.

About 11,000 years ago, when the last glacier receded and the rains of the southern lands diminished, man probably found his caves were not so convenient as they once had been. The hunter had often to roam long distances in search of game. He and his family needed portable shelters or ones that could be easily and quickly constructed. We know that this was so because he sometimes drew on his cave walls pictures of these portable shelters—summer homes, shooting boxes. And so the artificial shelter—the house—was born.

SNOW

As man had spent his entire sheltered life in caves, he naturally thought of his artificial shelter from the inside out, not from the outside in. He wanted to reproduce, as nearly as he could, the interior of his cave. And so he built that interior. He stood in one spot (sometimes he first dug out a large hole in the ground) and then piled up materials—stones or brush or skins —around him. For this reason, the first houses must have been round houses.

MATS

When man discovered farming and settled in one spot permanently or semi-permanently, his family expanded and he found his small round houses cramped. Of course, he could have built several individual round houses as separate rooms all joined into a compound. Many people still follow this kind of house arrangement. But if heat had to be conserved, if building materials were hard to come by, or if custom demanded one house per family, then one house it had to be. Man very quickly learned that rectangular houses could be made larger than round ones and that additional rooms could be simply tacked on when the need arose.

GRASS

Rectangular houses appeared early in the developing farming communities along the Nile and the Tigris-Euphrates Rivers. In those areas there were few trees other than occasional palms. Reeds grew thick and

EARTH

BARK

SKINS

fast, however, and apparently houses were built of
them. Houses are still being built of reeds in the Tigris-
Euphrates marshes, an area now part of Iraq. The reeds
are tied in thick columns and joined at the tops to form
arches which are then covered with reed matting.

Though reed houses were useful, even beautiful and
stately, they could not have been very good at keeping
out the wind, which blew through the holes. Eventually
another building material came into use. There was
plenty of it, certainly. It was mud. At first men probably just plastered over the reed matting. After each
rain or flood the mud had to be renewed. Brought to
the house in round-bottomed baskets, perhaps the mud
dried a bit as in a mold and was simply piled against
the reed matting in that form. If someone had a fire in
one of those reed-mud houses, they no doubt quickly
discovered that heat baked the mud hard and durable.
Though one can only guess, it could have been in just
such an accident that the ubiquitous brick—basic ingredient of huts and palaces—was created. It is true
that there was a time when Mesopotamian houses and
temples *were* built of bricks with rounded tops, something very like loaves of well risen bread. Eventually

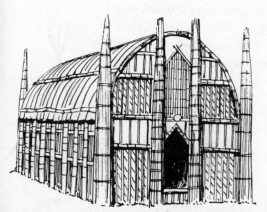

A SHEIK'S REED HOUSE IN
THE MARSHLANDS OF IRAQ

they were replaced by the simple, efficient rectangular brick. But for a long time, ancient builders included a few old-style bricks in each new-style building—sort of as a good-luck charm or perhaps as a reminder of the hallowed past.

As might be expected, beauty very quickly became as important as usefulness. The beautiful shapes of buildings counted, and the walls were awash with color. Not only paint, but glazed tiles adorned walls both outside and in, delighting the eye of the passerby and announcing the wealth and importance of the owners.

Let's go from walls to roofs. At first, as we have seen, the roofs were curved as in those Iraqi reed houses, or pitched against a central upright pole. But when the time came to build royal palaces, much bigger rooms were needed, and the curved roof tops were just not practical. The time came for beams and poles, which were covered with reeds and then plastered in the usual manner, making the flat-topped roof still so popular and useful in hot climates.

Later, men found that rooms could be larger and a heavy mud roof still could be adequately supported by using sturdy uprights—columns at regular intervals. The familiar, tightly tied bundles of reeds were handy, of course, and so was the palm tree. Both were used. Can you guess how we know? When men learned to make their columns of other materials, they made them in such a way as to recall those early houses, those first

STONE COLUMNS

columns. The stems of the reeds, the leafy tops, even the bindings which held the bundle together were faithfully translated into stone. You can still see these markings on the columns of many houses and public buildings today.

And there are other architectural echoes of the past. The pitched roofs of houses meant to shed rain or snow still recall the old first dwellings, pitched to a center pole. Arches of stone bring to mind those first arches of reed bundles bent together. Even today's many-storied building harks back to other such buildings invented when history had only just begun. The ancient Egyptian town house designed to provide the maximum amount of living space on the minimum amount of ground is one such example.

Man is sometimes as conservative about his houses and his dress as he is about his tools. It is as if he longed to hold on to his past. As if, for all his cries of "Onward! Upward! Progress forever!" he wanted to keep in his things, his buildings, his material life, a remembrance of his earlier self.

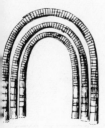

ARCHES OF REEDS

ARCHES OF STONE

THATCHED ROOF

PITCHED ROOF

11

RELIGION
Symbols for a Sense of Wonder

At the Vatican in Rome, you can visit the beautiful Sistine Chapel. Its walls and ceiling are covered with glorious paintings from the brush of Michelangelo, paintings which represent people and stories holy to the Christian faith. For it is a sacred place.

In the valley of the Vézère in southern France there is a cave called Lascaux. Its walls and ceilings, like those of the Sistine Chapel, are covered with beautiful paintings. They were put there by unknown artists, men who lived long ago during the last ice age. The meaning of the paintings can only be guessed at now. But we know Lascaux and caves like it were special, for no one ever lived there. No one could. Some of the painted caves are narrow, uncomfortable, dark, deep in the mountain's heart. Yet, men once came together in such

169

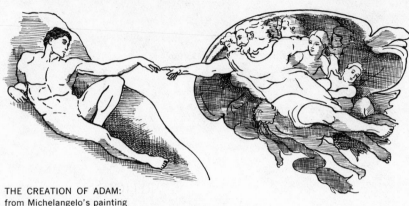

THE CREATION OF ADAM:
from Michelangelo's painting
in the Sistine Chapel

places, perhaps to worship, to recreate there images
and stories with holy meaning. If so, Lascaux too was
a chapel, a sacred place.

Blessed Mother Mary and the infant Jesus together
compose a picture dear to Christian hearts. Lady Isis
and the infant Horus were just as beloved among the
faithful of ancient Egypt. Both mothers are images of
love, the first love a child can know, the one he carries
with him through life.

The Christian cross recalls a supreme sacrifice and a
terrible death. But it signifies life, too, life eternal. So
once did other crosses sacred to men of other times,
other religions. The double ax of Crete, the Egyptian
Ankh, even the swastika (in spite of its recent sinister
association with the Nazi cause) once meant life and

joy. The cross seems always to have had special meaning. Enclosed in a circle—without beginning, without end—the cross is one of mankind's oldest religious symbols.

And that, in truth, is what the chapels, the madonnas, the crosses, the pictures all have in common. They represent in one form or another man's deepest, most complicated thoughts. His thoughts about himself, about life and death, about sickness, about the beginning of the world and his own place in it. In short, religious symbols put into understandable terms the things man finds most difficult to understand.

Alone among animals, man is supremely conscious —self-conscious and other-conscious, susceptible to beauty, given to dreams. Alone among animals, he knows of his own existence and of its destined end. Alone among animals, he asks, "Who am I? Why am I here? Where will I go when I die?" Alone among animals, he questions and he wonders.

If—in his raw beginnings—he had not turned up some satisfactory answers to his overwhelming questions, he might very well have lost both his newfound sense of wonder and his sanity into the bargain. But he didn't. Out of wonder and out of need came answers. They were answers based on what he knew of things around him, enlarged perhaps, awesome and terrible perhaps, but still within reach, still to be classified by his own definitions. It was simply a matter of describing what he did not know in terms of what he did know

ISIS WITH THE INFANT HORUS

—which is, in a way, what science still does. With answers, the powerful forces of nature, the animals or plants on which he depended for food, the way of life and death—all these things he could understand and, by understanding, seek to influence. At least he could rob them of their terror.

For example, when early man fell ill, did he fret himself to death wondering what had happened and what would happen? No, indeed. He thought of the sickness as a "something," an evil spirit, that could be cast out of his body. And so, in positive fashion, he summoned his local shaman, who then tried to determine whether the patient was the victim of "witchcraft"—of some enemy's malice—or whether a foreign substance such as a stone, a bat, or a mouse had invaded his body. In either case, the doctor found a way to remedy the situation—either by casting a counterspell or by removing the offending substance. Often he did this by a sleight-of-hand trick, palming a stone and exhibiting it later as a demonstration of his skill. Often the patient himself was aware of the trick, but it never bothered him any more than it did the doctor. The treatment accomplished what it had set out to accomplish: restoring the patient's confidence and peace of mind, which surely helped the body's natural healing processes to function. This very sort of healing is still being practiced in many parts of the world where modern medicine has not yet penetrated—and often where it has, in direct competition. For germs, these people say, are just as invisible as spirits but not nearly so soul-satisfying to remove.

Religious symbols—myths and images—not only helped man to understand and cope with sickness and with the world outside himself. They helped to explain his own mysterious being—his troubling dreams, his conflicts, his behavior; why he was at times compelled to do things he had not meant to do or say things he had not meant to say. This foreign, unknown stranger-self he personified as a demon or as witchcraft at work. We know now these strange reversals come from within us, but how comforting it would be, now and again, to shift the responsibility to some uncomplaining demon!

The same symbolic forms have a way of turning up all over the world, because human beings everywhere have always had similar dreams and similar troubles and similar joys. They are born and grow up in families and get old. They must cope with the loss of those they love as well as the prospect of their own death. In the memory of his dear departed, man's first and most persistent notions of continuity took form. For did not the family go on forever, and—living or dead —was not a man always a part of it? As an ancestral spirit he could look forward to honor from his descendants and to having a powerful hand in the management of their affairs on earth.

Groups of people living and working together have tended to develop a consensus of religious symbols and to settle on forms that mean the most to all. It is a kind of unanimity that helps people stick together and keeps them strong and solid. These common images and rites and myths, taken all together, express the special way of looking at life that makes each group of people different from all other groups—just as individuals differ, one from the other.

Each group uses its particular images, its religious ideas, to help soften the sorrows life brings and to heighten the joys, to set aside a part of life that will always be very different from the everyday world, that is especially precious, sacred. Each group also uses its particular images, its religious ideas, to sanctify tradition, to support it, and to keep it going. Children learn step by step that the good old ways are holy as well as proper. Among many primitive peoples, young men (and sometimes girls, too) are initiated into the group's traditions through awesome rites, often with painful mutilations whose scars they will forever bear along with the lessons pain teaches.

From need, then, and out of a sense of wonder, there came to man explanations of the world outside himself as well as of the world of his own dreams. Through need and wonder he found his place and his meaning in the universe, his place and meaning among men.

NEANDERTHAL
BEAR CEREMONY

The ability to wonder must surely be as old as man himself, but the first evidences we have of it are in the caves of Neanderthal Man. He shared his ice-age home with the giant cave bear who was, in milder weather, his enemy; in winter sleep, his food. In either guise, the cave bear must have represented something deeply important, something mystic and awesome to Neanderthal Man. In his caves have been found little shrines with bear skulls ceremoniously arranged. Perhaps we can find a clue to the meaning of these shrines in a ceremony still performed today among the Ainu of Japan, those white-skinned, hairy men, relicts of an earlier time, before Mongoloid people came to the Japanese Islands.

Men of Ainu villages bring baby bears home from wild places, rear them tenderly, feed them, play with them, and love them. When they grow into great bears, they are killed with much ceremony, their heads and skins arranged in shrines, and their souls sent home to tell the spirit-bear-parents how nicely they were treated by the Ainu and how much they would like to visit earth again, and again give up their flesh to be eaten.

Scholars think it likely that Neanderthal Man believed in a life after this one, for we find in his caves the bones of his loved ones carefully buried with things they used or loved in life: flint tools and horns of ibex and joints of meat to provide food for the dead on that last, long journey.

When we come to our own kind of man, *Homo*

sapiens sapiens, the evidences of religious belief are many. For these were the people who painted glorious animal pictures on the walls of their caves. Sometimes they left signatures, painting around their own hands (many with fingers missing) as if to leave a record of identity, as if to say, "See, I lived . . . I was here . . . this is my hand." Pictures of human beings are very few in these caves, and when they appear they are most often in animal dress—partly human, partly animal. Magical creatures they are: masters of the game beasts they lure and walk among without fear. For animals cover the walls of these cave chapels, animals of all kinds and in all conditions—leaping animals, wounded animals, animals with child. It was on animals that these primitive hunters depended for life itself.

Perhaps they thought of their gods as animals. Or perhaps they thought of the animals as undying spirits who must be induced to return, year after year, willingly to submit to the hunter, willingly to yield their flesh to the children of men. To lure back the animals, to re-create them in the body of Mother Earth, hunters painted animal likenesses on cave walls. To preserve the harmony of nature, the bonds of life between man and animal, they found sacred ways of speaking that were not like everyday talk. They imitated the bird's song and the wind's whistle, and found music. They moved in special ways not like walking or running but copied from the rhythms of nature—the stag's leap, the water's eddy—and thus found the dance. They acted

THE "SORCERER" OF THE
CAVE OF TROIS FRÈRES

out the sacred stories of their beginnings, of how the ancestors came; they showed to a watchful nature their needs and hopes—and thus they found drama.

Later, when man became a farmer, his well-being depended on the fertility of the soil, the abundance of the harvest, his life rhythms were attuned to the shifting seasons. Then his guiding spirits became symbolic of this new pattern for they were gods of the seasons, plant gods who yearly died and, like the plants, yearly were reborn. Often he worshipped earth goddesses, mother goddesses, because in them he saw the symbol of fertility, of increase, of the giving of life. And also perhaps because women may have been initially responsible for the discovery of agriculture.

THE BABYLONIAN
WAR GOD ADAD

As a farmer, but especially as a keeper of herds and flocks, man was a warlike creature, raiding the movable wealth of his neighbors, expecting to be likewise raided, and ever prepared to defend his own. He saw and admired the importance of the bull or stallion or ram in dominating the herd, and he came to worship father gods, warlike gods—gods who wielded lightning bolts, who shook the skies with thunder and made the earth tremble.

When one group of people overcame another, their gods were often conquerors, too. The vanquished gods had then either to go, quite literally, underground to be worshipped in dark and in secret as devils, or else—particularly when herding peoples and their gods overcame planting people and their goddesses—to undergo

FERTILITY GODDESS

wholesale celestial marriage. This is how the Greek and Norse pantheons with all their family groups came to be. After such a marriage, of course, the goddesses—like their people—were no longer supreme. But they generally found ways of evening the score, just as their human counterparts did down below.

Along with large populations and complex politics—especially with city living and all its problems of administration and order—came organized pantheons of gods, divine boards of directors, each god being responsible for a special department and having a special function. If you lost your purse, for instance, you prayed to the god of lost articles, who sometimes doubled as the god of thieves. Prayers for rain and prayers for love and prayers for success in a business venture all had to be addressed to the proper divinity to ensure immediate attention. Sometimes these city gods had special animal heads which told what their jobs were. Or perhaps these animal heads were a relic of hunting times, when people had identified themselves with particular animals.

It was often in the cities that great temples were built to honor the gods. In cities, too, men—especially men of wealth and power—took a giant step away from those simple cave burials with their sprinklings of red powder and the few relics the deceased had loved in life. Now men built gigantic tombs in which they hoped their bodies would be eternally preserved. And with them, into the other world, they tried to take all their wealth, all their comforts, even their companions —dogs to follow them, slaves to serve them, wives to love. Later on, clay figurines and painted pictures were used to represent the living creatures and were thought magically to become real in the afterlife.

To preside over all these temples, these tombs, to serve these many gods, and to guide the people through the proper ceremonies binding and preserving heaven and earth, there grew up vast priesthoods holding great power in the land.

Among hunters, one single wise man, the shaman, had been sufficient to their needs. He had interpreted the ways of gods and nature to his flock, cured their ills, presided over the rites that marked changes in their lives—when they ceased to be children, when they married, when they brought forth offspring, when they died. In those early times, men tried to placate hostile nature by properly performing the old rites, by paintings, by singing, and by dance.

In planting and herding times—perhaps because there were more people and life was cheaper—men added the element of human sacrifice. Sometimes, especially among planting peoples, human beings were regularly slain at certain seasons of the year to personify the plant gods who yearly died and yearly were reborn. Later, people would be sacrificed only in times of real disaster to avert the wrath of the gods. In the coastal cities of the Near East, parents immolated their most precious possessions, their children. Sometimes

THOTH, EGYPTIAN GOD OF
WISDOM AND OF THE MOON

kings themselves died willingly to purchase the well-being of their people, the fertility of the land, the favor of the gods.

For a very long time in man's history, people turned to religion to tell them how to get the good things in life and how to keep life good. They never dreamed religion could (or should) also tell them how they ought to treat one another. Then slowly this idea began to grow. On the walls of their tombs, Egyptian Pharaohs began to call the gods' attention to their good behavior in life, how nicely they had treated their subjects, how just they had been, how kind. Wise men and philosophers here and there about the ancient world started talking of right and wrong as something more than just convenient ways to keep the city peace, to make it easier for people to live together smoothly. Moses, the Hebrew leader, gave his people a code of behavior sanctioned by their God.

And then came the great teachers, one by one. The Buddha in India, Confucius in China, Zoroaster in Persia, the Hebrew Prophets, Jesus, and Mohammed. Life, all human life, they taught, is precious and to be cherished. And the righteous man is not necessarily he who lays up treasures in heaven, but he who minds his behavior here on earth. In many different ways, they all said much the same thing: do as you would be done by. We call this the Golden Rule. Perhaps it is a rule more disobeyed than followed, but men everywhere still feel it is a good rule to try to live by.

Notions of right living have come to be an insep-arable part of religion. But of the many ways in which man's capacity for wonder is expressed, not all have remained part of what is traditionally thought of as religion. An artist, for example, no longer confines his attention to divine subjects; he does not, like the paint-ers of the great caves or primitive artists everywhere, use his work to achieve magical results. But his art still grows out of feelings of awe and reverence for beauty and perhaps a flash of insight into the meaning of life. And, like his pious colleagues of ages past, he hopes his paintings will give others something of his private revelation. The singer no longer sings only church music, nor does the dancer necessarily interpret the ancient stories of creation. Drama is no longer chiefly concerned with divine intervention in the affairs of men. And it is the scientist, no longer the priest, who seeks to learn the secrets of the universe and of the world about us—the earth, the sky, the stars, and the beginning of it all. His answers are based on testing, trying, observing—not on dreams and not on guesses. And he learns early to accept the fact that tomorrow's observations may yet prove today's answers false.

Because of this separation of man's sense of wonder from his old religious habits, many people began to question religion. Or they felt there was a great chasm between what the scientists and artists said was true and what the old religious stories said was true. And they were either afraid or scornful.

But more and more men are coming to think that there need not be a chasm between the wonder of religion and the wonder of science. We have not changed. We are still creatures who seek and question. We have merely outgrown some of the old answers and we must look for new ones. We must find new symbols, new interpretations, to give us flashes of insight into the meaning of the universe and of the beautiful and orderly ties that bind us each to each, and each to All.

Actually, it is the scientists themselves who point the way. Any of them would tell you that when they earnestly seek the meaning of nature and of nature's laws, the answers they find are always far more beautiful, far more majestic, than anything they could possibly have imagined. And whenever they find the solution to one mystery, a larger one always presents itself. Some may never be solved until we can get out and away from this planet. Some we can never solve in this life. The important thing is the search itself. And in that search all men are brothers—from him who saw the wrath of God in the lightning to ourselves who seek our answers and our beginnings out beyond the solar system in the vastness of space.

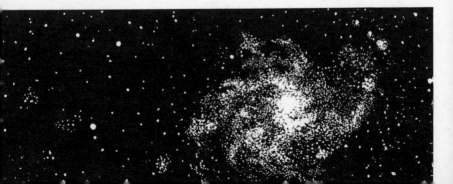

DOMESTICATING PLANTS AND ANIMALS
A New Meal Ticket and Time on Our Hands

You are what you eat. Everyone knows that if your diet lacks enough vitamins and minerals and proteins and carbohydrates, you will get sick. Or maybe you will just not be able to function as well as you might have with a well balanced meal under your belt.

Early man was what he ate, too. And he could eat a lot of things. Probably only the bear is equipped to consume the wide range of provender—animal, vegetable, mineral—that man can digest. It has been thought that those big nutcracker teeth of *Zinjanthropus* were especially adapted for chewing vegetable roots probably still gritty from the earth. Other early men whose very much smaller teeth have been discovered had, presumably, already made the transition to a largely meat diet. It is just possible that the new diet, so rich in protein,

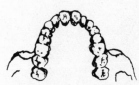

ZINJANTHROPUS   HOMO SAPIENS

helped account for some of man's physical changes. In any case, it did allow him to live in cold climates where other primates could not. And because small amounts of meat gave the same energy as large quantities of herbiage, he did not have to eat all day long. He could spend the extra time in hunting.

Even as a skilled hunter, however, life was still difficult for early man. Nearly every waking moment had to be spent thinking about where the next meal was coming from. This is reflected in the caves of later Stone Age Man, where pictures of animals cover the walls—real animals, super animals, animal gods—but animals, necessary to the hunter's survival. He ate when he could —the way animals do—gorging himself one day, going hungry the next. For he knew little of preserving foods and, indeed, most often had little left over to preserve.

Then he found a new way of life and a steadier source of food. And with this new source, man became one of the most numerous mammals on earth instead of the rarest. This new source of food was agriculture. Man domesticated plants. He caused them to grow where he chose, tended them to get the greatest yield, and harvested them when they were ripe. The plants, in turn, adjusted so to man that they could no longer grow wild and unattended. And not long after the invention of farming, certain animals—one-time prey of the human hunter—would be lured into the early farms to become tame beasts of byre and barnyard, as dependent on man for tending as his plants had become.

Some scholars have thought the discovery of agriculture might have been made along the seashore where man became a hunter of the waters as well as a hunter of the land. Since food from the sea in some form or another is usually plentiful, man could have settled there more permanently and had greater time in which to explore the surrounding land with its foliage and growing things.

Whether this is the way it happened or not, it is certainly true that man had always been a food gatherer. Berries here, a raided beehive there (as his rock pictures tell), some succulent roots dug up with stick or stone. Even when he became a hunter, he did not completely give up his gathering habits. He just turned the job over to his wife.

It was a perfect job for her. While man had always to be free to fight and chase and kill, she was nearly always encumbered with babies and could not participate in the active life. However, with carrying slings to bind an infant to her back, she could be free enough to wander and to gather what foods she found. Armed with a digging stick—a simple shaft weighted with a pierced stone, perhaps—she made the rounds of the countryside near camp. The digging stick is still used in many primitive farming communities and still recognized as a woman's implement.

Woman became the first botanist. She learned the characteristics of many growing things—which were good to eat and which were not, which kept well over

MAN GATHERING HONEY
(from a Spanish rock drawing)

long periods, which would make a person sleepy or even cure an ailment. And she taught this lore to her children. At the family hearth she became a chemist, too. It was probably she, as keeper of the flame, who learned that cooking made the starchy grain food edible, that even some of the poisonous plants could be rendered harmless by heat.

The idea of actually planting rather than simply gathering what grew wild certainly did not come all at once. Perhaps an observant woman, returning with her wandering band to an old camp site, noticed that the root leavings she had thrown on the refuse heap last autumn had sprouted anew. We know that there were once Indian tribes on the North American continent who did not plant grain but who returned to the same place yearly to harvest the wild seeds. Others planted corn and even fertilized it by burying fish with the seed. But they did not cultivate the fields. They went away after planting time, returning months later for the harvest.

PAPUAN WOMAN WITH
A DIGGING STICK

Out of assorted customs such as these, the idea of agriculture took root and grew. Some scholars believe the idea was first put to *intensive* use somewhere in the Fertile Crescent, that is, the arc of green that stretches up the Tigris-Euphrates river system, across Palestine, and down the Nile. Other independent centers of agriculture appeared later around the world—in Middle America, in West Africa, in Southeast Asia between Malaysia and the east coast of India. But many people think the idea may have spread outward to these centers from the Fertile Crescent.

Though the first intensive farming probably developed along the river systems, the first *farms* themselves appeared in hill country above the river valleys of the Fertile Crescent nine thousand years or so ago. There grew the wild grasses which would later become domesticated wheat and barley. Their grains could be stored safely away against lean seasons and, when cooked, made a starchy, filling, nourishing food. In other places, in the Congo basin, for instance, or in

THE FERTILE CRESCENT

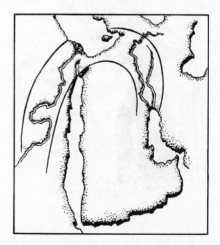

Southeast Asia, the damp forest environment did not permit cereal crops to grow. There people came to depend on starchy root crops such as yams and taro, or starchy fruits such as banana and breadfruit. In the Americas, the Indians domesticated the native maize (corn to us) as their main starch food.

The slopes of what is now upland Iran were, in many ways, perfect for the very first farms. There were no forests to be cleared away, and there was (at first anyway) plenty of rain. For a long time woman probably continued to be the chief farmer—as she still is in many primitive farming communities today.

But as the work grew heavier, the fields more extensive, and hunting less and less important, men began to lend a hand. At first they probably only helped occasionally with the reaping, or with fencing and rough hoeing as they do in some African tribal farms today. With more advanced farm tools, with farm animals to be taken care of, and especially after the plow was in-

KARAMOJONG WOMAN
USING PRIMITIVE HOE

vented, men assumed the major share of the work. For a long time, however, the responsibility for the planting remained with the women. There was, people of those times thought, some mystic connection between the fertility of women and the fertility of the earth. In a good many early farming communities, women indeed assumed a greater importance than they would have in later times. Ownership of land was often vested in the mother's family, and men took the name of their mother's rather than their father's clan. All this may have been a reflection of woman's early expertness in the ways of planting—her importance in the magical rites connected with planting. It may be simply an outgrowth of even earlier ways of organizing family life. We do know, however, that in all the places where early farming people once lived, unfailingly there are found quantities of fertility figures, little goddesses of stone and unbaked clay. It is from such humble beginnings that the great mother goddesses of later times would emerge—Isis of Egypt, Demeter of Greece, Inanna or Ishtar of Mesopotamia, and Ceres of Rome, from whose name we get the very word *cereal*.

With farming, people could at last settle down to a fairly permanent life. In the beginning, the farmer (he or she) probably continued to live in his cave home, commuting to the fields below. Later he built villages of those round houses we spoke of earlier. These were still only *fairly* permanent abodes because man still had

CLAY GODDESS OF EARLY
FARMING PEOPLE IN IRAN

to move occasionally. He knew nothing about fertilizing his fields, and when their productivity was exhausted, he had to pull up stakes and move on to new
land and build a new village. This is, perhaps, one reason why the river valleys along the Tigris-Euphrates
and the Nile came in time to attract many, many farmers. Although these river lands were marshy and had
to be drained and laced with irrigation canals, they
were inexhaustibly fertile. This was because the rivers,
overflowing in flood, deposited fertilizing silt on the
fields. Farmers could stay put on their lands, they and
their children after them.

As a result of farming, many ways of life changed.
Meat ceased to be the staple food. People found ample
protein in their coarse, cracked, boiled wheat and in
the milk products from their goats and sheep. What
was lacking in vitamin B, they may have found in their
yeasty beer. For alcoholic beverages seem always to
have been an immediate result of man's conversion to
farm life. People lived longer, too, for toothless old
folk now had soft, nourishing porridge to eat. No
longer the burden they had been to hunting bands,
which were hungry and in danger and always on the
move, old folk were now valued for their wisdom and
for the stories they could tell about the past.

Baskets and pottery were invented, for, with a permanent address, people could afford to accumulate possessions and extra food. They could even keep drinking
water conveniently in the house. Pottery made all these

things possible. And remnants of those old pots and jars are still opening up possibilities for today's archaeologists. You wouldn't ordinarily think of ceramic ware as being particularly durable—and it isn't, somehow, in dining room or kitchen (especially if it happens to be your best china!). But in the ground it is practically indestructible. Even if it lies there in bits and pieces, these pieces last and can be restored to their former shape. The colors and designs on ancient pottery, the geographical distribution of these designs, and the earth levels at which various types of pottery are found help set the age of a settlement and tell us something of its connections with other settlements, near or far.

Most of all, as farmers people had more time. Some seasons were less busy than others, and at the end of the day, there was time to chat, time in which to be bored and to wonder what to do with themselves. From this extra time came many new activities.

A great elaboration of religious rites was one immediate result. Colorful rites were real diversions from the everyday monotony of a settled-down life. People responsible for the rites, the priests, multiplied and specialized. Particular buildings were set aside for them and for the gods they served. Sometimes these buildings, always larger and more imposing than ordinary houses, were right in the village. In the uplands, they were sometimes located in a ceremonial cluster, all alone—like big shopping centers today—and the outlying farmers trooped in for the glorious holy days.

Often the farmers gladly spent all their extra time in the building of temples and ceremonial centers.

Early farmers who lived along the rivers began to venture up and down stream. Something better than floating logs or inflated pigskins—meant simply to get a body over the water and onto the opposite bank—was needed, and boats developed. First, perhaps, came rafts of logs or reeds tied together and commended to the river's current. Later came poles and oars and sweeps. Canoes made from felled and hollowed-out trees are known among primitive people the world over —in places, that is, where there are trees for the felling. Elsewhere boats are made of reeds, complete with gunwales and curving prows, just as they must have been in ancient times. Last of all came sails—one of man's first attempts to harness the natural powers around him.

On their sailing journeys, men encountered other village-bound people like the relatives they had left at home. Perhaps these new people needed grain or something else the sailors' village had to offer. The men on the boat and the men ashore exchanged goods; they traded. Soon people began to develop tastes for exotic trade items that had to be brought really long distances. Not always things that had real utility, but novelties, rare colored stones, even rarer metals were desired. Adventurous rivermen took to trading as a full-time occupation. And little by little, the horizons of settled villagers were stretched to cover a wider world.

Farming was not the only way of life to provide a more secure food supply than hunting ever could. There were other people who lived out on the great grass plains of Central Asia and on what was then the grass plain of the Sahara. The people who lived in these places had learned to manage herds of animals—cattle and, later, horses, in Asia; cattle, sheep, and goats on the Sahara plains. Later, after the last retreat of the ice, after the Southern rains diminished and the desert came, camels would be domesticated. Away up north appeared a people who followed great herds of reindeer. All these nomads lived lives dependent on their herds. They ate their flesh, drank their milk, made tents and clothing from their skins. Cattle people who live today below the Sahara also drink the blood of their animals, preferring this to killing them for meat. For cattle are precious to these people, almost sacred.

Nobody is entirely decided about just how the domestication of animals began, but nearly everyone agrees on the first animal domesticated. It was the dog, and apparently he became man's best friend not long after man became man. Australia, when it was discovered by European explorers, contained only two placental mammals: man and dog, both having arrived long, long ago by raft or boat on that lost continent of ancient marsupials.

Perhaps the friendship between man and mutt started when wild dogs hung around a hunter's camp waiting

A HUNTER WITH HIS DOG
(from a Spanish rock drawing)

for handouts or to scavenge. As dogs proved useful in the hunt, perhaps the handouts increased. In time, some dogs became tamed and, preferring the company of man, grew dependent on him. These dogs were able to reproduce in captivity or in proximity to man (most wild animals are not). Because of dependence and separation from his wild cousins, the dog's appearance changed considerably. This is true of other domesticated animals as well, animals which were taken into man's company for their meat or milk or hair or muscle.

There are many rock drawings, from Scandinavia to Africa, which show man with his friend the dog. Apparently the dog was used, as he is now, for protection, as a watchman, and as a companion, as well as for his help in the hunt.

As for the domestication process itself, it seems clear that man never started it with an eye for the practical —at least, not in the case of animals other than the dog. It may have begun this way. A hunter killed a mother animal. Then he saw her baby, so helpless and appealing. He thought of his own children and took the baby animal home to be a playmate and a pet. The practical uses occurred later when the helpless baby grew up into a surly adult. Into the cooking pot with him! So anthropologist Ralph Linton sees the sequence.

It may also have happened that in time of drought and hardship, wild sheep and goats were lured to farmers' planted fields. Perhaps they were allowed to glean through those fields after harvest and thus became accustomed to the presence of man. It is certainly plain that some barnyard animals quickly became necessary features of every early farm, valued for their hair and milk as much as for their meat and hides.

The hunting people who one day became herders of the plains may, indeed, have taken the idea of domesticating animals from their planting neighbors. But this still does not quite explain how man learned to manage herds of large, wild cattle. It is more likely that, in such cases, he simply shifted from following wild herds (the way our Plains Indians followed the buffalo) to guarding and finally to herding them. Never entirely tame, they learned to tolerate and depend on man. Early

CATTLE HERDERS (from an
African rock painting)

cattle men who occupied the Sahara Desert, then a sea of grass, painted on cliff walls perhaps the most graphic record ever of the herding life.

It is a way of life very different from that of the farmer. Herders move frequently with their animals in search of fodder. They learn to travel fast and to travel light. Because their wealth is on the hoof and in the open, it has always been a temptation to poorer men. There were cattle rustlers in the very early days of herding even as there were in the American West. Raiding all too quickly came to be a kind of game. Men bragged about how many cattle (or horses or sheep or camels) they had cut out from an enemy's herd. They got used to raiding and being raided and soon became tough and resourceful warriors as well as skillful herdsmen.

When these hard, quick fighting men came into contact with settled farming people, they said "hello" with more raids because that was their way and all they knew. This time they took away, not cattle, but gold and surplus grain and slaves. Farming people were never much of a match for hungry plainsmen and often got much the worst of it in a fight.

This sort of contact became more and more frequent as the great grasslands began to dry out. The Sahara cattlemen moved into the Nile Valley or down into lower Africa. Some groups of Arabian herdsmen moved to the coastal settlements or those of the great river basins. Some remained behind and became adapted to a truly desert existence. The people of the Central Asian Plains learned the use of the wheeled cart, which they harnessed to their native horses and rolled over the Danube into what is now Europe. In many places they encountered cities already old in civilization. And civilization was still another way of life, as different from the ways of both village and plain as each differed from the other.

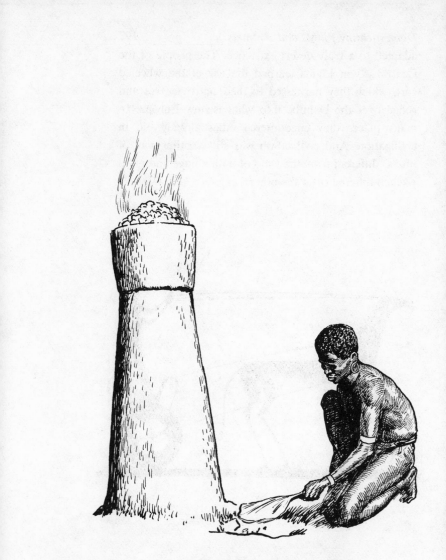

SUDANESE SMITH SMELTING IRON

13

METALS REPLACE ROCKS
Enter Gadgets and Machines

With the spread of the new way of life—the new, easier abundance of food—man had time on his hands. Time to think, to try, to experiment, to discover. As we have seen, trading expeditions were one result of the new life. Trade brought in exotic items from far away, items that were not just useful or pretty but that were often thought to have magic power, power to bring health and good luck. Among these were metal nuggets from the rugged slopes of Anatolia and the various gem stones, such as turquoise, malachite, and azurite.

Man had long had a nodding acquaintance with metals. He had treated pure nuggets as better, though rarer, stones—and certainly stones with magic properties to boot. He had chipped the nuggets, ground them, polished them. He had even discovered that they possessed a marvelous quality which true stones do not:

they could be pounded cold into a variety of shapes; they were malleable. He quickly learned to use them as ornaments.

Of course, it never occurred to him that these "rocks" would melt or, better still, could be cast. This he discovered in the roundabout way by which most great discoveries are made. He learned that metal would melt at the same time that he learned something even more startling: that it could be got out of yet another rock that bore not the slightest resemblance to the metal itself. From the beautiful blue azurite and the sea-green malachite came copper, ruddy-orange and gleaming. Here is how it might have happened.

First of all, malachite and azurite had uses other than as gem stones. Ground up on palettes, mixed perhaps with fats or other binders, they made a very satisfactory paint. The early Egyptians especially were fond of anointing their eyelids with malachite paint. They found it offered the eyes some protection from the burning sun. Ground malachite (because of its copper) also was a kind of disinfectant against the eye diseases from which these people suffered.

Now let us imagine a typical New Stone Age gentleman (of perhaps 7 or 8 thousand years ago) on a short trip away from his farming village. As Professor Ralph Linton tells the story, our man has been on a stone-collecting expedition to the hilly, ore-bearing regions near what is now Turkey. Loaded with a satisfactory haul, he starts off home, dreaming of brisk trade in prospect. Overtaken by darkness, he stops to build a fire and settles down for the night. The wind is blowing quite hard, whipping his flames this way and that. He leans over to add another stick when suddenly his gem-laden pouch falls off his belt and into the fire, made extra hot by the bellowing wind. He rages and tries to retrieve the burning pouch. Too late. Imagine his astonishment when, next morning, he finds his pouch burned away and, in its place, a little puddle of copper —that already known, already prized "stone."

Or perhaps it was a potter who made the original discovery when, leaning one day over his kiln, he accidentally dropped his paint jar full of malachite "eye-shadow" into the heat below. No matter. Given enough episodes like these and the march of metals would have been well under way.

The greatest demand for metals must have come from the river-bottom lands, mud lands into which even the stones had to be imported. The people of these lands would have immediately appreciated the copper tools, which outlasted those of stone and which, when blunted, could be resharpened or even recast. What an economy of time and effort!

Experimentation with every likely-looking ore must have soon turned up, besides copper, silver, lead, and gold. Experimentation with firing disclosed the best ways of applying heat in stone and clay furnaces. The clay crucibles which held the ore allowed the left-over slag to collect at the top. The molten metal at the bottom could then be tapped. At first the liquid metal was allowed to cool and harden in open stone molds. One

COPPER SPEAR
AND AX HEAD

half a blade or spear point resulted which could later, with heat, be fused to its twin, ground, polished, and sharpened. As the skill of smiths improved, they learned to make the desired object in the round and all at once in a single pouring. They modeled the object in clay, patted on wax, added more clay on top, and baked. The wax then melted and ran out of a hole at the bottom, leaving a hollow mold into which the molten metal could be poured. When this cooled and hardened, the clay was broken off, leaving a perfect, finished product. By this method (the "lost wax method") many beautiful art works were produced.

Copper, the principal everyday metal for spear points, daggers, plowshares, and pins, was very soon found to have its own disadvantages. Though better than stone in some ways, it was not really hard or durable enough to suit ever more demanding tastes. And so smiths began to mix copper with other metals to get better results.

Again this knowledge probably came about by accident. All the ores were impure. Alloys nearly always occurred naturally. It was only when men learned how to get purer grades of copper that they also learned that the old, impure copper ore had really been better after all. And so they began mixing deliberately. Best of all the mixtures was copper and tin, which yielded the wonderful hard bronze for which a whole age has been named—the Bronze Age (about 3000 to 1250 B.C.).

The great cities which grew up on the Tigris and

COPPER OFFERING STAND FROM KHAFAJE

Euphrates Rivers depended on bronze. So, too, did the cities on the Nile and the developing civilization in the Aegean world. Bronze was a big factor in warfare, both in defense and offense, for metal weapons were clearly superior to stone ones in the thick of battle. Leaders who could accumulate a good store of metal arms stood a very good chance of dominating enemies and becoming war lords.

Copper and tin are not the most common of metals, and soon the great cities sent their ships out questing around the known world for sources of ore. The ships, especially those of the maritime powers, grew bigger and better; seamen became bolder and more skilled in navigation. Ships of the Aegean traveled as far as the British Isles, whose tin mines insured their popularity. The imprint of a Mycenean dagger, for example, has been found on one of the stone pillars of venerable Stonehenge, a circle of great stone uprights that may have been a kind of astronomical observatory. Perhaps the dagger was the signature of the Aegean architect who helped erect the monument, or the mark of an ordinary trader leaving behind his own "Kilroy was here."

Traders even went as far as the Scandinavian settlements which, having developed a craving for ready-made bronzes, traded their amber in return. The cities of Sumer (the Mesopotamian birthplace of civilization) traded with sister cities in India. And an Egyptian queen sent her ships coasting down Africa as far as

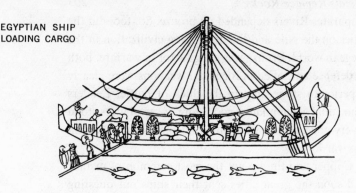

Punt (Ethiopia, some think this was) to bring back wonders.

And then one day the era of bronze trading came to an end. Sometime after 1250 B.C. the trading ships ceased to leave port, copper mining dwindled, the smelters cooled. This happened when a new metal, a better metal, came into general use: iron.

Actually it was not a *new* metal. The Egyptians had long known it as "the marvel from heaven," obtainable from fallen meteorites. And they had treasured this rare commodity for use in the most sacred of their ceremonies, the opening of the mouths of the dead so that they could magically consume the symbolic food left behind in their tombs and thus live forever.

When the feverish experimentation with ore-firing was in progress, surely iron ore was tried—and discarded. The smelting problem was just too great. The ore required much higher temperatures than could easily be produced by furnaces used for smelting copper. The ore had to be fired with carbons in just the right amount. And even after all that effort, the metal still did not liquefy. It formed instead into a spongy mass which had then to be pounded while white-hot to force out the slag—rather like wringing out water from wet clothes. And that was not all. The cast iron often proved to be brittle, more brittle than bronze—hardly worth the trouble. So must have run the thinking among smiths of the Fertile Crescent.

It took another people, a people unused to bronze, outsiders really, to learn to get iron of good quality. Their iron was better than bronze. And with weapons made of it, with the horse-drawn chariot, they entered the Fertile Crescent by way of Turkey and came to be well-nigh invincible there. These were herding people, the horse and cattle people from the plains of Central Asia.

There are still people today who smelt iron in furnaces very like the first ones ever used. They are the Jur, a tribe of Sudanese smiths. Their knowledge of ironworking came to them (by way of Ethiopia) from the Egyptians—who got theirs from the conquering Assyrians (around 650 B.C.)—who got theirs from the Hittites, proprietors of a considerable empire in what is now Turkey, who were first to use the metal extensively. The Egyptians had tried to get it directly from the Hittites when the two countries were at war with

EGYPTIAN SMITH

each other (around 1250 B.C.). It was perhaps the most successfully kept military secret of its day. And the Egyptians, missing the opportunity then, simply discarded all notion of iron-using until several hundred years later.

With the advent of iron—and also because of the widespread disturbances caused by the invasions of the herding peoples—the bronze traffic stopped. Iron ores are pretty common everywhere. And people who had depended on foreign trade for their metals began smelting and using the iron in their own back yards. Suddenly everybody had metal and lots of it. And the Iron Age was born.

While metals were coming into important use, man turned his hand to several useful gadgets which were to have far-reaching consequences for our own time— one especially, the wheel. Some people still think of it as a kind of turning point in man's history, with everything lumped in a before or after category. It was probably not that earth-shaking. After all, great cities in Middle America and ancient Peru functioned without wheeled vehicles. It was not that the wheel was unknown there; it was simply used in children's toys. With the jungles around and, in Peru, the precipitous moun-

SUMERIAN WAR CHARIOT

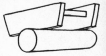

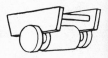

tains, the people there probably could not have used the wheel even if they had wanted to or known how. In our civilization, however, the wheel is basic to a great many activities besides transportation. Without it, we could not have machinery, for example, or turbines for the manufacture of electricity. In the old days, the water wheel made irrigation possible. Harnessed to water or wind, wheels ground corn. The potter's wheel made possible large, beautiful, and mass-produced ceramic ware.

No one knows just when or where the first wheel was invented. Pictures of very ancient wheels were found in royal graves in Ur, a large Sumerian city, and are dated at about 3000 B.C. As they were even then quite sophisticated, the wheel must have come into use much earlier. After 3000, the wheel spread rather quickly around the Fertile Crescent and up to the herders of the plains—except for one place. Egypt was just as slow about getting the wheel as about getting iron. Wheeled vehicles did not appear in Egypt until after invasions by the desert folk, about 1750 B.C. Before then, pyramids, temples, monuments—all were built without wheeled carts or wheeled pulleys. Huge stones were dragged on sledges to the building site and wrestled into place by manpower alone. Sometimes the way of the sledges was made easier by rolling them on logs placed one after another in front of the sledge as it moved along. It was probably from this combination of sledge and log that the idea of the wheel originated.

But oddly enough, it never happened in Egypt, conservative Egypt.

When the wheel and sledge came together in the cart, men found ways to make their domesticated animals do the pulling. Harnesses were invented. Early ones fastened around the neck, half choking the draft animal and certainly reducing its efficiency. Not until a long time later would this situation be corrected.

Oxen were probably the first animals in harness, then the onager, the little donkey native to Mesopotamia. The plainsmen of Central Asia, having picked up the notion of wheeled vehicles from Mesopotamia, used their native horse as a draft animal. The introduction of this splendid charger into the ancient city-centers of civilization was one happy result of the plainsmen's invasions of the area.

The metal-tipped plow was also a useful invention of those times and, like cart or chariot, it was harnessed to an ox or an onager—or occasionally a wife. With the plow, larger fields came under cultivation, and greater food surpluses were produced. Though this farm implement can be considered the most utilitarian of all man's inventions, its early uses may not have been practical at all. Some scholars think the plow may have appeared first in religious ceremonies celebrating the time of seed planting.

The loom came into being soon after women learned

to twist wool or flax into thread. They must have done this first by rubbing the fibers together on the bare thigh as many Eskimo women, even today, twist sinew strands. Later came the whirling spindle and much, much later the spinning wheel.

The first threads were woven into fabric much as baskets and mats are woven—in and out, out and in, with the warp threads perhaps pegged down securely. Eventually ways were found to pull the sets of alternating threads apart so that the weaving thread could be shot through all at once and the job done faster.

The first real textiles were discovered in early Egyptian farming sites. Flax grew abundantly in the area, and linen became the fabric preferred by the fastidious Egyptians, who considered wool not only hot but ritually unclean as well.

Not so the desert people to the east whose herds of sheep and goats provided fibers for yarn. Wool yarn was woven on upright looms, brightly dyed, and made into cheerful articles of dress like the coat of many colors worn by Joseph.

Flax does not dye well and so, for much of their history, Egyptians had to content themselves with surgical white enlivened when possible by jewelry. White though it was, however, and woven on cumbersome horizontal looms, Egyptian linen was the finest cloth the world has yet seen. So fine it was, so transparent, with threads so tightly woven that, even with our best machines, we have never succeeded in duplicating it.

14

WRITING
Capturing Yesterday for Tomorrow

None of us today gives much thought to our writing. Not to the "how" of it, at any rate. After a brief, first-grade struggle with signs and symbols, we get caught up in the meaning and style of written words and forget the mechanics of putting them on paper. Learning to write is relatively easy, and in the Western world, nearly everyone *can* write. It was not always so, and among many peoples it is not so yet. There are those who have no opportunity to learn and those who cannot spare the time it takes to learn a complicated system of writing. Learning to write Chinese, for instance, is no easy matter. To acquire a passable education you would have to learn at least 3000 different symbols, each of which stands for a word. To be a real savant, you would need to be able to recognize and write over 40,000. How different from our system, which permits us to reproduce the *sounds* of all our words with just twenty-six letters—the wonderful alphabet.

Of course, man did not start out writing with a ready-made alphabet. In fact, writing did not start out looking like writing at all but something else instead. It started with pictures. Everyone likes to draw or at least doodle, and we have been doing both for a long, long time. You remember how late Stone Age Man painted on the walls of his caves. Wondrous pictures he made, magical pictures to give him power over his animal quarry or to offer to his animal gods. Sometimes he left his own handprints with the pictures, or even mystic symbols whose meaning we shall never know.

Later he began to want to draw himself—to remind people who came after him that he and his tribe had once been on a great buffalo hunt or had surrounded a herd of giraffe or fought a fierce battle with bows and arrows. These pictures were not so beautifully detailed as the drawings in the cave chapels, nor so sacred, but they were full of life and action. Man found he could tell real stories in pictures. It was a way of putting his mark, his signature, on life. It was a way of preserving yesterday's ideas for tomorrow, of giving them continuity, of making them live. There had always been

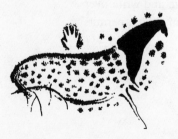

HANDPRINT OF A
STONE-AGE ARTIST

this kind of magic about pictures. It was a magic that would carry over into writing.

Now there is much that the simple memory of man can do to capture the past. Among many peoples without writing, specialists arose whose job it was primarily to remember. By keeping track of the names of kings, for example, a good deal of tribal history could be recalled. (The African king of Dahomey went about as far as you could go in the matter of memory specialists. He assigned one to each of his councilors. Human file cabinets they were, responsible for keeping a mental record of all agreements, negotiations, decisions.) Because verse is easier to remember than prose, traditional lore was often recounted in this form, sometimes to musical accompaniment. Many parts of the Old Testament and all of the *Iliad* and *Odyssey* were handed down in this fashion for centuries before at last breaking into script.

But even with memory nudgers such as verse or quipus (those colored and knotted cords used by the Incas), the human mind alone could not encompass all of man's accumulated and growing knowledge. The important historic events would be retained, perhaps, but not those everyday observations without which conclusions cannot be reached, without which science cannot develop, without which city life on any scale is difficult. In order to build on the past for the future, man needed writing. And he got it.

The idea of writing grew straight out of that picture

doodling we have been talking about. And it began, most scholars think, in the Fertile Crescent (fertile, it would seem, for so much more than grain)—specifically, in the mud flats of Mesopotamia. Pictures and, later, picture writing came to be many things to many people—a system of magic, a record of history, a vehicle for religion. To the Mesopotamians, its chief use was in business—at first, at any rate. And because their picture writing was first engraved on stone and later on clay baked hard, we have an unusually complete record of its development. A sample of what is thought to be the oldest known writing in the world was found in Kish. Carved on limestone (about 3500 B.C.), it was perhaps the property of a businessman of one of the Sumerian cities in Mesopotamia. He may have used it as a kind of identification tag, a signature. When he wanted to mark something "personal"—a jar of oil or barley—or to set off the boundaries of his property, he dropped a blob of wet clay on the lid of the jar or on the wall marking his land and then pressed his seal stone onto the wet clay, leaving his signature for all to see. (We still do just this sort of thing, but only on official documents.) The signature might be a picturization of his nickname or of some brave deed he had accomplished or of his place of residence. In any case, the first pictures used as writing stood for actual things. A boat was a boat, complete in all essential details; a man was a man, and the more the sign looked like the original, the better. Later, instead

LIMESTONE TABLET FOUND AT KISH

CYLINDRICAL STONE WITH ITS CLAY IMPRESSION

of flat seals, craftsmen made little cylinder seals which one rolled over the wet clay, leaving a longer, more descriptive picture behind.

Eventually, thing-pictures proved very limiting. They were fine for simple stories, stories which would identify the main events in a man's life, say. A boat, a stone, a star might mean: He owns a boat in which he transports stones by starlight. Plain enough. But suppose our man is not a simple man or a happy one. Suppose he wants to tell about taking a journey during which he suffered many hardships. Suppose he wants to pray to the gods that such experiences will never come his way again. What then? He might use the ordinary thing-signs to mean something more. Maybe the boat could stand for the journey; the stone could represent hardship; the star could become a word for gods. And this is exactly what did happen in the early days of writing. The thing-pictures became idea-pictures which enabled man to write more fluently than he had before.

In addition to giving a man his mark, Mesopotamian picture writing was also used in its beginnings for taking inventories of goods. This was especially helpful in the big temples where records had to be kept of the presiding deity's net worth in lands and grain and copper knives and domestic animals. Writing was useful, too, in consummating foreign business deals, in buying and selling and keeping a record of the returns. For the people of lower Mesopotamia, a land without metals, without wood, without stones even, had long since

SOME EARLY SUMERIAN IDEA-PICTURES

picture:	star	bowl	foot	eye
meaning:	god, sky	food	stand, go	see

learned to depend on trade. Hardheaded businessmen, they were, merchants, exporters, and traveling salesmen.

In Egypt, on the other hand, all the land belonged to the king, who was the god on earth, not simply the god's steward as was a Mesopotamian king. And all early Egyptian writing is concerned with the king as god. The Nar-Mer Palette (c. 3200 B.C.) is one of the oldest samples of just such royal publicity. It also documents an important event in early Egyptian history— the merger of "the two lands" into one. The king of the south (confusingly known as Upper Egypt) is pictured with club upraised in the act of braining his enemy, the king of the Nile delta. The southern king is much the

THE NAR-MER PALETTE

most imposing figure in the scene, larger than his rival, his patient sandal bearer, or the corpses of marsh-landers underfoot. The episode is blessed by divinity, for two heads of the goddess Hathor, part cow, part woman, look on while Horus the hawk god leads captives on a leash.

The Nar-Mer Palette tells us something else, too. This earliest of all known Egyptian writings is already sophisticated enough to use puns, or sound-signs, for spelling out names. Such a system is called rebus-writing. It still turns up constantly in word games and bad jokes. A rebus is a picture that says one thing but means another. The classic example combines the pictures of a bee and a leaf to express, not something animal and vegetable, but something abstract: "belief." A rebus accompanies every figure in the Nar-Mer Palette. The one over the king's head is enclosed in a large house (which is what "Pharaoh" meant) and includes a fish (*n'r*) and a chisel (*m'r*)—Nar-Mer. (Egyptian hieroglyphs, by the way, took no notice of vowels.) The unfortunate enemy seems to be named "Washi" (harpoon, pool). And the captive of Horus bears on his cough-drop-shaped torso six lotus blossoms, which are not there for beauty's sake but to indicate the total number of prisoners taken. The word for "lotus" (*kha*) also meant a thousand.

Because Egyptian writing in its earliest bow is already pretty fancy, many specialists believe that the *idea* of writing came to Egypt from Mesopotamia.

HAWK GOD HORUS
WITH HIS CAPTIVES

Sumerian writing is clearly older by several hundred years, and all its stages—from the first crude pictographs to ideagraphs to rebus—are very well documented. No such background has yet been unearthed for Egypt. For much the same reasons, scholars wonder whether the Mesopotamian idea of writing stimulated a similar development sometime later in cities along the Indus River (in what is now Pakistan), in the Hittite lands, on Crete, and in China. But if the *idea* was borrowed, that seems to have been all. Certainly it was all that traveled across the desert from Mesopotamia to the Nile, for the two ways of writing were very different indeed. They served different purposes from their beginnings and their forms are very different, too. This may have been due, at least in part, to the different writing materials used. The later Greeks called Egyptian writing *hieroglyphika grammata,* "carved sacred letters" (from which we get "hieroglyphics"), and, in a way, this phrase describes it well. While it is true that the Egyptians wrote on other things (notably a paperlike material made from beaten papyrus reeds), they wrote first on stone and with the greatest possible elegance and grace. And certainly they dwelt on religious themes.

Mesopotamian writing was done on the material most ready to hand: mud, the universal ingredient of temples, houses, and pots. Baked hard, it was almost imperishable. Now, when you write on clay, time is of the essence because if you pause to ponder, your writing surface hardens and you are out of luck. Laboring overlong with your art may also give you hardening of the drawing board. It was inevitable that someone would discover a shorthand method of rendering the pictures—a method that would save time and work and clay, to boot. This is how it worked.

If you tried to draw pictures of a moth and a butterfly (without models to go by), you might be hard put to find a way of distinguishing the two until you remembered the antennae. That is something to capitalize on, for the butterfly's antennae are knobbed stalks while those of the moth are like feathers. If you had to do this often—if, in fact, it was the only way you could communicate on the subject (and you *might* be interested if your clothes were motheaten and your garden covered with butterflies), you would soon find yourself drawing only knobs and feathers and leaving out the rest. This is just the sort of thing that happened to writing methods long ago. The outstanding features, the distinguishing features, of each picture were retained and stylized. Eventually, one could hardly recognize the original picture in the final sign.

In the process of time saving, so especially important to the business communities in Mesopotamia, not only did scribes stylize the symbols, they began making them in a totally different way. They stopped drawing and began stamping, for which purpose they used the cut end of a reed. It made a little triangular mark which gave this kind of writing the name it has borne ever

EVOLUTION OF "FISH" IN SUMERIAN WRITING

| earliest form | turned around | 2500 B.C. | 2000 B.C. | after 2000 B.C. |

since its first decipherment about a hundred and fifty years ago. "Cuneiform," it is called, from the Latin word *cuneus*—a wedge.

The Egyptians, too, very soon began to transpose their stately glyphs into shorthand script. In some ways it is rather like the difference between printing and handwriting. The script has been called "hieratic" (of the priests) and this is a very accurate description. Because Egyptian writing began in the service of sacred matters, because of its difficulty and the time needed for education in its use, writing was an art confined for a long time to the priestly classes. They acted, not only in their capacity of ceremonial ministrants, but as clerks, stenographers, and civil servants, too. And writing was surrounded by an aura of mystery. It was a skill not to be revealed save to the chosen few.

Later the priestly group was expanded to admit boys of wealth or promise who could spend the many years required in the temple schools. These educated ones were known as scribes and were very much respected and admired in Egypt. Wealthy or aristocratic men were proud indeed to have themselves portrayed as scribes. With the extension of learning, hieratic script itself was simplified to what we call "demotic" (of the people), though this term is a bit misleading because not everyone could write.

In the use of signs for sounds, both Egyptian and Mesopotamian writing made progress. It was the next step up from puns—pictures that said one thing but

meant another—to plain syllables. To the Egyptians
this was just an extra element to be added to an already
crammed symbol vocabulary. Not so for the Mesopotamians, who were ever on the alert to short cuts. They
began to use a syllabary altogether, limiting the clutter
of picture and idea signs. This meant that their lexicon
of symbols could be reduced from several thousand to
several hundred.

Only certain spoken languages, actually, lend themselves to this kind of reproduction. They have to be
languages with easy, simple syllables containing one
consonant and one vowel each. Old Sumerian was such

FROM PICTURE TO SCRIPT IN EGYPT	HIEROGLYPHIC	HIERATIC	DEMOTIC
eagle-owl sound-sign for *m*			
sound-sign for *y* in word endings			
thing-picture meaning "lion"			
idea-sign for "lotus pool"			
category sign for words dealing with birds or insects			

m + n

n + f + r

a language and so today are Hawaiian (*Ka-me-ha-me-ha, a-lo-ha*) and Japanese (*Yo-ko-ha-ma, sa-yo-na-ra*). Hawaiian never had its own system of writing, but Japanese has long used syllable-symbols. English is not an easy language to render in syllable-signs, for our syllables very often combine more than one consonant with a vowel sound (*ex-act-ly, strict-ly*).

The confusion in ancient Egyptian writing was further compounded by the omission of vowel sounds. Syllable-signs might stand for two consonants (*m.n*) or even three (*n.f.r*), and the reader had to guess what went in between. Semitic languages (Hebrew, Arabic) are still written in this way. In addition to the syllable-signs, the Egyptians had also evolved a system of single sound-signs, an "alphabet," really. But it never occurred to them to use these signs in a truly phonetic method of writing. They simply tacked sound-signs (whether single or in syllables) onto the original idea-gram, which then became a kind of category signature telling whether the word dealt with an animal, human, or divine subject; its shape, size, occupation; gender, number, and mood. There were hundreds and hundreds of such determinatives in written Egyptian. (One is reminded of the Bantu spoken languages, which do the same kind of labeling in a verbal way, with prefixes). A spelled-out word might be capped with one or several category signs as in "hungry man." Or an idea-sign might just stand alone, with or without a determinating picture. It was entirely possible in Egyptian

"HUNGRY MAN" IN HIEROGLYPHS

sounds
h·k·r
hungry

sign
for
hungry

sign
for
man

idea-signs alone   sound-signs + idea-sign

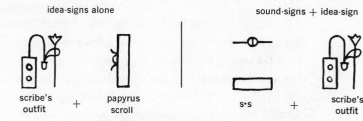

scribe's   +   papyrus   s·s   +   scribe's
outfit   scroll   outfit

writing to render a single word in several different ways in the same sentence and feel perfectly comfortable about doing so. And that is not all. A document might very well contain, not only different methods of writing, but different scripts as well. For the Egyptians never abandoned the ancient hieroglyphs. They were reserved for all the "best," the most sacred, the most important subjects. A scribe might therefore start his scroll with a paragraph in hieroglyphics, follow this with a few lines of hieratic explaining some points of less import, and add some notes at the bottom in demotic.

The invention of a totally simplified form of writing was made by another people, a people caught halfway between cuneiform and hieroglyphics and wedded to neither; a people who had little to unlearn and even less to lose by trying something new and different. The alphabet began, some scholars think, at a particular time, in a particular place. And from this single invention all the alphabets of the world would later develop. This could have been the way of it:

The Egyptians had a number of valuable copper and turquoise mines on the Sinai peninsula. These mines

LATE EGYPTIAN SOUND-SIGNS FOR CLEOPATRA
(enclosed in a royal ring, or cartouche, and
capped with category signs meaning female)

were usually worked by slaves, but sometimes the wandering herdsmen of the area would ask for employment. Like the people who would be known as the Hebrews, like the Phoenicians of the coastal cities of Palestine and Syria, like the Arabs to come, these people spoke a Semitic language. Being voluntary workers, they were willing workers and clever and industrious workers, and the Egyptians were happy to give them jobs. Some of them even became foremen of mine shafts or overseers of one sort or another. They were then required to keep records for their employers. But tally lines scratched on rocks and accompanied, perhaps, by crude picture-figures certainly made for inefficient records to say the very least. The Egyptians often wished to teach these men to write. But how could they teach men who could barely speak Egyptian all that formidable system of picture-writing? Impossible.

Then someone—perhaps one of the workers—hit on a brilliant plan. Why not borrow the Egyptian picture-signs and use them for Semitic words? Someone else remembered that Egyptian picture-signs sometimes stood for single sounds. Better and better! Borrow a picture. Let it stand for a Semitic word. But then (and here is the clever part) *use* only the initial sound of that word in writing. One might take the Egyptian picture for *ox,* call it *aleph,* and in writing have it represent the sound *ah.*

However the system got started, it must have worked because archaeologists have discovered a good many crude alphabetic inscriptions in the area. Some are cut into rocks and some, of a clearly religious nature, are engraved on little goddess figurines. Perhaps they were meant to be permanent prayers with much the same motivation that prompts church-goers today to light candles and donate shrines. One inscriber used writing in the same way that Stone Age Man left his painted handprint on cave walls: to leave a personal mark on the world. His words have been interpreted as "I, the badger [miner], foreman of mine shaft number two."

It may be that the alphabet was invented elsewhere in Syria-Palestine. Perhaps it happened in Byblos, a coastal city whose famous cedars had long been sought by kings and builders the world over and whose merchant princes had many Egyptian contacts—and contracts. (For it is agreed that our alphabet derives from Egyptian models.) In Byblos there was also a good deal of experimentation with syllabaries based on hieroglyphs and applied to a non-Egyptian tongue.

The notion of an alphabet, in fact, seems to have been "in the air" at the time—probably sometime between 1800 and 1500 B.C. It was a period of disturbance and upheaval in that coastal strip between great Egypt and great Mesopotamia—a time ripe for new thought and new invention. A true alphabet using cuneiform symbols was unearthed in the port city of Ugarit (now called Ras Shamra) in Syria. And there have been found in several Palestinian sites fragments of alphabetic script looking something like the Sinaitic

STONE WITH SINAITIC WRITING

signs, something like later Phoenician signs, which may
have been derived from it.

What is certain is that the alphabet was invented by
people speaking a Semitic tongue and that right away it
was put to the service of common people. It appeared
on ordinary trinkets and potsherds and carried quite
ordinary messages and motivations. No longer the ex-
clusive property of priests and scribes and wealthy merchants, the alphabet made learning available to the
many instead of the few. It revolutionized knowledge as
iron had revolutionized technology.

The Phoenicians quickly adopted the alphabet, so
useful in trade and business, so efficient for record keeping. The signs had changed now from the crude pictures of Sinai. By those shorthand processes we have
discussed before, the pictures were stylized until they
were no longer recognizable as pictures. They grew
neater, quicker to write. And because they were written
horizontally across the writing surface instead of up
and down on it, the signs were turned to suit the new
direction.

The Phoenicians took this system of writing to the
Greeks, who had lost their old knowledge of writing
during barbarian invasions. The Greeks, being just as
quick-witted as the Phoenicians and maybe a bit more
imaginative, took the new figures, changed them
slightly, and added signs for the vowel sounds so important in their language. The Greeks stopped writing
back and forth across the page—"as the ox plows,"

they called it—and began writing from left to right
only. And the letters changed accordingly.

Greek colonies in Italy gave the alphabet to the
Romans. Some think it may have taken a more circui-
tous route, traveling from the Greek cities to the Etrus-
can cities and *then* to Rome. The Romans, too, modified the letters to suit their language. It is the Roman
form of the alphabet which we use today, and most of
the Western world along with us. Russia has a modified
Greek alphabet, called "Cyrillic." Hebrew and Arabic
letters derive from earlier pre-Phoenician forms, as do
the alphabets of India.

HIEROGLYPH	SINAI SYMBOL	PHOENICIAN	GREEK	ROMAN
ox	aleph—ox sound: *ah* aleph	aleph	alpha	A
house	beth—house sound: *b*	beth	beta	B
door	daleth—door sound: *d*	daleth	delta	D
snake	nahas—snake sound: *n*	nahas, or nun	nu	N

LAND GATE AT ASSUR

15

CIVILIZATION
The Icing on the Cake

In the first five chapters of Part II we assembled all the basic ingredients of human culture. Culture, of course, does not mean just appreciating opera or visiting art museums or holding a tea cup with the little finger properly crooked—though these are undeniable minor elements of our *own* culture. Culture—with a capital *C*—is what makes man different from all the other living beings on this earth. It is his ability to attach conscious, abstract meanings to the necessities of life and to teach these meanings to his children. It is his ability to think (forethought and afterthought, as well as thought in the present); to use his hands to make things to a purpose and a plan—things meant to give him protection or comfort or beauty; to communicate with symbols (vocal or drawn or written); and to wonder. These abilities are Culture, and these abilities have produced Culture as expressed in tools, in planned societies, in language, in clothing and shelter, and in religion and art. And these basic cultural inventions are common to all humanity everywhere. The rest is icing on the cake. But what icing it has come to be!

There are no human beings without language, without family structure, without shelter, without religion, though some still live by hunting and gathering and use stone tools in the process. People can farm without the plow (and many do). People can transmit tribal lore without writing (and many do). People can move about without the wheel (neither car nor bicycle has totally replaced foot power). Yet, without food surpluses made possible by the plow, without quick transportation made possible by the wheel or by the boat, without writing with which to leave permanent records behind, there would never have developed that ultimate complexity we know as civilization. Generally regarded as man's crowning achievement, it is certainly the latest, if not the last, addition to man's basic cultural repertoire.

It is hard to say *exactly* what civilization is because it is really nothing new. It includes all the basic inventions, plus the farm economy, metals, technology, and writing, all enormously magnified, refined, and elaborated. At its greatest extension, civilization becomes itself man's environment instead of his response *to* the environment. A civilized man, for example, can live without ever seeing the fields which produce the food

he eats. And he can gain a knowledge of life from
books written about it by other men. I suppose one
might say that civilization is really a grace note on the
song of all that went before. It is life at a faster tempo
and in a louder voice.

But if it is difficult to say exactly what civilization is,
at least we know where it started. It began in cities. All
the words describing this kind of life tell us that. The
very word "civilization" comes from the Latin *civitas,*
which means "of the city-state." From that root word
we get "civics," the study of government; "citizen," a
participating member of the (city) state; "civic," anything to do with the (city) state. The corresponding
Greek root word is *polis*—the city. From this we get
"politics," practical ways of achieving government;
"politician"—everybody knows what that means; "po-
lice," originally those who enforced order in a city;
"policy," a plan of government action; "metropolis,"
the mother city, the big city. And "megalopolis"—the
big, big, *big* city. Another Latin word for city was *urbs,*
which is now our "urban," of the city; "suburban,"
adjacent to the city; "exurban," *way* outside the city.
From *urbs* comes also "urbane"—a quality of sophisticated behavior characteristic of the city-dweller—the
city slicker, if you will. And from *civitas* comes "civil,"
the behavior of a man who knows how to conduct himself in a city—polite, knowledgeable, *civilized*.

This is the key—"civil" means "of the city." And the
city is civilization. Now, cities (and the civilizations
they produce) are not all alike. The Mayan cities in

Central America (at their height in 800 A.D.) were mostly temple cities, ceremonial centers which the local population visited on special holy days. In these temple cities lived the astronomer-priests who, being freed from the necessities of earning a living, devoted their time to learning, experimenting, and leading the people in the new ways and ideas they had discovered. Certainly, the setting apart in some way of particularly bright and responsible people does seem to help provide the informed leadership without which progress cannot take place. But the setting apart takes place in differing ways among differing peoples.

Egyptian civilization seems to have grown, not from temple centers or separate and rivalrous cities, but from one long ribbon of humanity stretching down both banks of the Nile. It was, I imagine, rather like the ribbon city lining U.S. Highway No. 1 all the way from Boston to Philadelphia—but with palms instead of billboards. Egypt's loyalty was concentrated first in its villages, then focused directly on the kingdom. At first there were two—Upper Egypt and Lower Egypt. The unification of the two lands into one signaled the beginning of Egyptian history and Egyptian civilization. All national feeling was personified in the figure of the god-king, as were the fertility of the land and the realm's mystic harmony. The many African kingdoms below the Sahara reflected this Egyptian model for centuries, until the arrival of European explorers and colonists imposed another prototype.

Our own Western civilization, however, grew out of cities whose brawling political life and problems and vitality and concerns seem to us jarringly familiar, even today. These were the mud-flat cities of Mesopotamia. Over-crowded, forever at odds with each other, forever in search of order, their civic innovations have, by way of many a cultural brook, swelled the river of our own civilized heritage.

Cities mean, first of all, people, and lots of them all concentrated in various spots. Now, people cannot bunch up together without food to make their staying possible. Even if they are drawn to a locality because of its magical or religious significance—because a shrine is there or a fetish or some other token thought to bring health and luck—they cannot remain there permanently if the land is barren. The mud flats of Mesopotamia were extraordinarily fertile, yielded several harvests a year, and could support a large population. But the fields had first to be wrested from the river marsh, dried and drained, and then irrigated properly. This kind of work could not be performed by individual

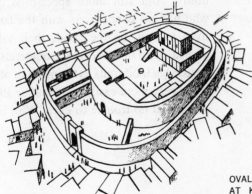

OVAL TEMPLE
AT KHAFAJE

families but required the labor of many men all working together. Naturally, for efficiency's sake, someone
had to direct the operation. Because—as we have seen
—priests were the first group of specialists to be set
apart from the rest of men, because they were thought
wise and close to the gods, they were first to take charge
in the god's name—whichever god happened to be
paramount in the particular area.

On those rich fields, more grain grew than could be
consumed, and much of the extra was taken as the god's
share and stored away in the temple treasury. It fed the
priests, of course, but, at their direction, it could also
be used to feed other budding specialists—laborers or
artisans—who spent their time on building projects for
the gods or in carving sacred statues or amulets. In this
way, the ranks of the nonfarmers grew. They tended to
collect around their place of work, putting up their
homes there. Others came to attend to *their* wants and
to those of visiting worshippers.

In time, the specialists turned their attention to more
secular pursuits, for there were well-to-do farmers
anxious to trade their produce for objects of beauty or
utility. And still more specialists appeared—people
who had no connections with the temple at all, who
lived entirely on the goods their talents or services
earned. With the appearance of metals, money replaced
perishable food stuffs as the medium of exchange. Silver
coins were more easily hefted, after all, than a brace of
goats, and no trouble to keep. With judicious lending,

they could even be made to multiply. It is no wonder people began to think of the new money more in terms of "mine" than of "His" (referring to the local deity, of course). Temple gifts no doubt began to decline, and the burgeoning cities felt the pinch. Perhaps then began that system of taxation which has followed civilized man so persistently as to become itself a kind of natural force. "Death and taxes," we are still wont to sigh, lumping together the two ultimates in inevitability.

As more and more specialists did less and less of their own farming, they came to be dependent on the farms lying at an even greater distance as the city limits spread. There could be, in fact, no city at all unless the food from these farms could be brought to the hungry urbanites. It is no accident that most of the great city civilizations have grown up along rivers. There was Egypt along the Nile, the ancient Indian centers of Harappa and Mohenjo-Daro along the Riva and the Indus, Shang China cities of the Yellow River, and the cities of Mesopotamia—the "land between the rivers." The river was the food life line to the city.

The river was also the trade life line out. The mud-brick cities of Mesopotamia were particularly dependent on trade—almost from their very beginnings. As we have seen there was no metal to be had in Mesopotamia, and no flint either. There were not even ordinary stones for axes. All had to be imported from the mountains upriver. And so the Mesopotamian businessmen were early versed in trade.

It was thus with most early cities—to a greater or lesser degree. In a city's first beginning, it is true, there must be a certain closed-door quality to the new way of life in the making. Shut off by deserts or mountains, confined to their own little island of fertility, the people pool their labor, use the thinking of their own specialists, and make a little culture entire unto itself. But very quickly each little entity must break its bonds and seek out fresh ideas or it ceases to grow. It is trade that brings a fresh outlook, satisfying man's eternal craving for something new.

At least one early city owed its entire existence to trade. Ancient Jericho—be-ringed by walls at least five thousand years before Joshua's trumpet blast—began by having the supreme attraction in a dry land. It had an inexhaustible spring and a shrine to the deity who kept its waters flowing. In time it profited greatly from the pack trains traveling both east and west, carrying ideas and goods overland between Mesopotamia and Egypt.

If cities traded with each other, they frequently had less friendly relations, too. They envied one another's riches, longed each to assert its own superiority—just as individuals play social "oneupmanship"—and often went to war. War, too, is a way of introducing new ideas. Quicker than trade, it nevertheless brings in its wake a misery and destruction that trade does not.

War brought to the Mesopotamian cities new ways of transportation and a quick testing of new weapons.

SUMERIAN SOLDIERS CHARGING THE ENEMY

It also brought a new order of rule. War lords supplanted the priests in leadership, often taking over many of their ceremonial functions. In each Mesopotamian city, the chief or king (*lu-gal,* "great man") was accounted the god's steward, responsible to heaven for the proper management of his city here below.

These new kings right away had many problems to contend with. There was, first of all, the population explosion and the necessity of preventing dissension among people crowded and crammed within the city walls. A city is not like a village, in which everyone knows or is related to everyone else. In a village, the authority of the elders, the headman, and most of all, the weight of tradition serve to keep mischief-makers in line. But, says Linton, city folk are strangers, caring little for one another or for public opinion. (And this was as true of Ur as it is of New York.) Furthermore, newcomers to the city are apt to be one of two sorts of people—those who are too bright, too energetic, too talented, to be kept down on the farm, or those persistent scamps whose home villages refuse to keep them. In order to forestall the explosions bound to occur amidst such flammable human material, Mesopotamian city rulers promulgated rules and regulations. They appointed policemen to enforce the rules and judges to decide when the rules had been broken and who was wrong in a dispute. Even the punishments for each sort of rule-breaking were predetermined, so the judges had, at least to a certain extent, to be fair.

These law codes grew so extensive that finally writing was pressed into service, and the codes were incised on stone and set up prominently for everyone to see. This was helpful for all the city newcomers who arrived with their own village standards and did not know what was expected of them. To give the laws greater authority—the kind of authority traditional village rules have automatically because they evolve in a family context—the king often had himself portrayed receiving the laws from the god. At the very least, the pictures on the stone pillars dramatized the god's approval of his king-steward and of the city's rule.

Writing soon came to be useful, too, in keeping track of people—their numbers, the taxes owed, the lawful transfer of their private properties in sales and by bequests.

The search for order here below was further sanctioned by the newly discovered order of the spheres above. And the gods themselves were thought to be organized in hierarchies of rule just as the cities were managed below. Priestly observers, watching the heavens night after night and noting their observations in writing, discovered a celestial predictability which permitted them to make accurate calendars. By means of the calendars, the correct dates for great feast days could be determined, the right seasons for sowing and for reaping, and—so they thought—the fate of human beings in life.

Other forays into science proceeded apace. Doctors

BABYLONIAN KING RECEIVING LAWS FROM THE GOD

—first as priests, then as ordinary professionals—experimented with surgery and drugs to help people keep well and to get well under the crowded, unsanitary city conditions. Builders developed mathematics and architecture and engineering. Merchants sought standardized weights and measures. And the scribe polished his learning and his script. So did the city grow.

What is true of the Mesopotamian civilization is, in many ways, true of all. All civilizations—whatever the sort of city from which they sprang, whether temple center or mercantile center or ribbon of villages and estates with urban knots scattered along the skein—all civilizations have certain effects in common. All civilizations support *specialists*. No one family lives totally independent of any other. The food producers in civilizations depend on the specialists for government services, manufactured items, entertainment, education, medicine, and ceremony. And all the specialists depend on the farmer for food and on one another for services.

All civilizations have *rules and laws,* sometimes (at least in the mercantile cities) embodied in written codes. All civilizations have some kind of government whether it comes from kings or priests or priest-kings or even popularly elected representatives.

All civilizations have some form of keeping records. All but one (the Incas had only quipus) developed some system of *writing*.

All civilizations develop *art* forms—literary forms,

music, dance. All civilizations find some means of passing on their achievements, of *educating* at least their most promising children if not all children.

All civilizations have *complex religions* with a well-regulated priesthood. Indeed, the very growth of civilization seems tied up in the growth of religion. In the beginning, it is very often the priests, the sacred brotherhood, who try out ideas that secular men will later follow.

All civilizations develop the *sciences,* whether as primarily practical expedients or to serve primarily religious ends. The form taken depends on the main interests of the society concerned. And these can be very different.

For as individuals differ, as languages and religious beliefs differ, civilizations themselves can develop very different personalities. Each looks at life a little differently from all others. Each gives first importance to different values, looks up to different heroes, develops along different lines. And each meets, in the long run, a different end.

What new inventions lie ahead for mankind? We have, it is true, discovered air travel and soon we shall have space travel to other planets, and perhaps even homes under the seas. But, marvels that they are, these are still only vast extensions of man's old urge to venture and to try and to get where he is going as fast as possible. From the thrown spear to the dropped bomb is a big step, too, though the basic idea as well as the intent is clearly the same. It remains to be seen whether these new technological advances will alter the basic way of our civilization, whether they will trigger changes in our values, in our ways of thinking and behaving.

At least it is clear that the headaches of the ancient city continue into our own time. The basic problem of keeping the city order and keeping the city peace remains the same. Only the city has grown. It has grown in population and in size. The civilization of cities has spread—even as it did in early times—to include first warring nations, then warring empires. It is likely that in time our smaller and smaller world will share one civilization—will be, in fact, one world-city, one megalopolis. And still with the same old problems. How to keep the city peace. How to keep the city healthy and happy. How to give to every citizen his due. How to use each one's talents to further both his own individual growth and the city's glory. How to be more civilized. How to be, not simply human and urban, but urbane and humane at last.

From a long, long line of animal ancestors we came—bone and flesh, hide and hair. Yet, with mothering, with teaching, by the use of hand and eye and brain,

we exchanged that animal world for another. It was a world begun with tools, a few words, and a dream. And as our new world expanded, we dreamed different dreams, spoke different tongues, struggled, and altered as our numbers grew. We congregated in cities and traveled from them afar. We learned and accumulated learning, and even found learning great enough to discover our own beginnings and imagine our own end.

In time we may leave this narrowing earth and tour the stars—stars and their circling planets one by one. Perhaps there we shall meet beings so vastly unlike ourselves as again to prompt the questions "Who are you? What are you?" Perhaps they will tell and we shall tell, and in the telling find one another more alike in mind than in body, united in a kind of humanness quite beyond flesh and bone and hide and hair—beyond learning, beyond experience, beyond fear.

And so we are not yet at the end of our story. Human life has only just commenced and will go on to new beginnings. For, as the poet Robert Frost has said, we have

> . . . promises to keep,
> And miles to go before we sleep,
> And miles to go before we sleep.

BIBLIOGRAPHY

Chapter 1: Climbing Our Family Tree

Berkner, Lloyd V., and Marshall, Lauriston C. "A New Theory of the Development of the Origin of Atmospheric Oxygen." *The New York Times.* Sunday, October 25, 1964.

Berrill, N. J. *Man's Emerging Mind.* New York: Dodd, Mead, 1955.

Eiseley, Loren. *The Firmament of Time.* New York: Atheneum, 1962.

Howells, W. W. *Mankind in the Making.* Garden City, N.Y.: Doubleday, 1959.

Hoyle, Fred. "Can We Learn from Other Planets?" *Saturday Review.* November 7, 1964.

————. *The Nature of the Universe.* New York: Harper and Brothers, 1950.

Merrell, David J. *Evolution and Genetics.* New York: Holt, Rinehart and Winston, 1962.

Penfield, Wilder. "The Physiological Basis of the Mind." In *Control of the Mind,* Part I, ed. by S. Farber and R. H. L. Wilson. New York: McGraw-Hill, 1961.

Rogers, Terence A. *Elementary Human Physiology.* New York: John Wiley, 1961.

Romer, Alfred Sherwood. *Man and the Vertebrates.* Baltimore, Md.: Penguin Books, 1957.

Simpson, George Gaylord. *The Meaning of Evolution.* New Haven, Conn.: Yale University Press, 1950.

Smith, Homer W. *From Fish to Philosopher.* Garden City, N.Y.: Doubleday, 1961.

Swanson, Carl P. *The Cell.* Englewood Cliffs, N.J.: Prentice-Hall, 1960.

Von Bonin, Gerhardt. *The Evolution of the Human Brain.* Chicago: University of Chicago Press, 1963.

Chapter 2: Man Among the Primates

Biegert, Josef. "The Evolution of Characteristics of the Skull, Hands, and Feet for Primate Taxonomy." In *Classification and Human Evolution* (hereafter cited as *Classification*), ed. by S. L. Washburn. Chicago: Aldine, 1963.

Devore, Irven. "A Comparison of the Ecology and Behavior of Monkeys and Apes." In *Classification*.

Goodall, Jane. "My Life Among Wild Chimpanzees." *National Geographic*. 1963. Vol. 124, No. 2:272-308.

Goodman, Morris. "Man's Place in the Phylogeny of Primates as Reflected in the Serum Proteins." In *Classification*.

Hooton, Earnest A. *Man's Poor Relations*. Garden City, N.Y.: Doubleday, 1941.

————. *Up from the Ape*. New York: Macmillan, 1947.

Howells, W. W. *Mankind in the Making*. Garden City, N.Y.: Doubleday, 1959.

Reynolds, Vernon. "The Old Man of the Woods." *Natural History Magazine*. 1964. Vol. LXXIII, No. 1:44-50.

Schaller, George B. *The Mountain Gorilla: Ecology and Behavior*. Chicago: University of Chicago Press, 1963.

Simons, Elwyn L. "The Early Relatives of Man." *Scientific American*. July 1964. Vol. 211, No. 1:50-62.

Simpson, George Gaylord. "The Meaning of Taxonomic Statements." In *Classification*.

Von Bonin, Gerhardt. *The Evolution of the Human Brain*. Chicago: University of Chicago Press, 1963.

Yerkes, Robert M. and Ada W. *The Great Apes*. New Haven, Conn.: Yale University Press, 1929.

Chapter 3: Man Among the Mammals

Bourlière, François. *The Natural History of Mammals*. Trans. by H. M. Parshley. New York: Knopf, 1954.

————. *Mammals of the World: Their Life and Habits*. New York: Knopf, 1955.

Colbert, Edwin H. *Evolution of the Vertebrates*. New York: Science Editions, 1961.

Eaton, Theodore H., Jr., *Comparative Anatomy of the Vertebrates*. New York: Harper and Brothers, 1951.

Fenton, Carroll L. and Mildred A. *The Fossil Book*. Garden City, N.Y.: Doubleday, 1958.

Newell, Norman D. "Geology's Time Clocks." *Natural History Magazine*. May 1962. Vol. LXXI, No. 5:32-44.

Prosser, C. Ladd, and Brown, Frank A., Jr. *Comparative Animal Physiology*. Philadelphia: W. B. Saunders, 1962.

Romer, Alfred Sherwood. *Man and the Vertebrates*. Baltimore, Md.: Penguin Books, 1957.

Smith, Homer W. *From Fish to Philosopher*. Garden City, N.Y.: Doubleday, 1961.

Westall, T. S. "Mountain Revolutions and Organic Evolution." In *Evolution as a Process,* ed. by J. Huxley. New York: Collier Books, 1963.

Young, J. Z. *The Life of Vertebrates*. Oxford: The Clarendon Press, 1955.

Chapter 4: Man Among the Vertebrates

Augusta, Joseph, and Burian, Zdenek. *Prehistoric Animals*. Trans. by Greta Horn. New York: Spring Books, 1960.

————. *Prehistoric Reptiles and Birds*. New York: Spring Books, 1961.

Berrill, N. J. *The Origin of Vertebrates*. New York: Oxford University Press, 1955.

Buchsbaum, Ralph. *Animals Without Backbones*. Chicago: University of Chicago Press, 1957.

Buchsbaum, Ralph, and Milne, Lorus J. *The Lower Animals*. Garden City, N.Y.: Doubleday, 1950.

Colbert, Edwin H. *Evolution of the Vertebrates*. New York: Science Editions, 1961.

Eaton, Theodore H., Jr. *Comparative Anatomy of the Vertebrates*. New York: Harper and Brothers, 1951.

Romer, Alfred Sherwood. *Man and the Vertebrates*. Baltimore, Md.: Penguin Books, 1957.

Smith, Homer W. *From Fish to Philosopher*. Garden City, N.Y.: Doubleday, 1961.

Young, J. Z. *The Life of Vertebrates*. Oxford: The Clarendon Press, 1955.

Chapter 5: Man Among Men

Ashley-Montagu, M. F. *Culture and the Evolution of Man.* New York: Oxford University Press, 1962.

Brace, C. Loring. "The Fate of the 'Classic' Neanderthals: A Consideration of Hominid Catastrophism." *Current Anthropology.* February 1964. Vol. 5, No. 3:3-37 (with comments).

Campbell, Bernard. "Quantitative Taxonomy and Human Evolution." In *Classification and Human Evolution* (hereafter cited as *Classification*), ed. by S. L. Washburn. Chicago: Aldine, 1963.

Coon, Carleton S. *The Origin of Races.* New York: Knopf, 1962.

Dobzhansky, Theodosius. *Mankind Evolving.* New Haven, Conn.: Yale University Press, 1962.

Hockett, Charles F., and Ascher, Robert. "The Human Revolution." *Current Anthropology.* June 1964. Vol. 5, No. 3:135-65 (with comments).

Howells, W. W. *Mankind in the Making.* Garden City, N.Y.: Doubleday, 1959.

Leakey, L. S. B. "Adventures in the Search for Man." *National Geographic.* 1963. Vol. 123, No. 1:132-52.

————. "Exploring 1,750,000 Years into Man's Past." *National Geographic.* 1961. Vol. 120, No. 4:564-89.

————. "Finding the World's Earliest Man." *National Geographic.* 1960. Vol. 118, No. 3:420-36.

————. *The Progress and Evolution of Man in Africa.* New York: Oxford University Press, 1961.

Mayr, Ernst. "The Taxonomic Evaluation of Fossil Hominids." In *Classification.*

Schultz, Adolph H. "Age Changes, Sex Differences, and Variability as Factors in the Classification of Primates." In *Classification.*

Simons, Elwyn L. "The Early Relatives of Man." *Scientific American.* July 1964. Vol. 211, No. 1:50-62.

Simpson, George Gaylord. "The Meaning of Taxonomic Statements." In *Classification.*

Washburn, S. L. *The Social Life of Early Man.* Chicago: Aldine, 1961.

Chapter 6: Man in Time

Buchsbaum, Ralph. *Animals Without Backbones.* Chicago: University of Chicago Press, 1957.

Campbell, Bernard. "Quantitative Taxonomy and Human Evolution." In *Classification and Human Evolution,* ed. by S. L. Washburn. Chicago: Aldine, 1963.

Colbert, Edwin H. *Evolution of the Vertebrates.* New York: Science Editions, 1961.

Ericson, David B.; Ewing, Maurice; and Wollin, Goesta. "The Pleistocene Epoch in Deep-Sea Sediments." *Science.* November 6, 1964. Vol. 146, No. 3645.

Ericson, David B., and Wollin, Goesta. *The Deep and the Past.* New York: Knopf, 1964.

Glaessner, Martin. "Pre-Cambrian Animals." *Scientific American.* March 1961. Vol. 204, No. 3:72-94.

Leakey, L. S. B.; Napier, John; and Tobias, P. V. "A New Species of the Genus Homo from Olduvai Gorge." *Nature.* April 4, 1964. Vol. 202.

Newell, Norman D. "Geology's Time Clocks." *Natural History Magazine.* May 1962. Vol. LXXI, No. 5:32-44.

Simons, Elwyn L. "The Early Relatives of Man." *Scientific American.* July 1964. Vol. 211, No. 1:50-62.

Chapter 7: Tools, Weapons, Fire

Burkitt, Miles. *The Old Stone Age.* New York: Atheneum, 1962.

Cole, Sonia. *The Prehistory of East Africa.* New York: Macmillan, 1963.

Coon, Carleton S. *The Origin of Races.* New York: Knopf, 1962.

Goodall, Jane. "My Life Among Wild Chimpanzees." *National Geographic.* 1963. Vol. 124, No. 2:272-308.

Hooton, Earnest A. *Up from the Ape.* New York: Macmillan, 1947.

Howells, W. W. *Back of History.* Garden City, N.Y.: Doubleday, 1954.

Leakey, L. S. B. *Adam's Ancestors.* New York: Harper and Brothers, 1960.

————. "Adventures in the Search for Man." *National Geographic.* 1963. Vol. 123, No. 1:132-52.

————. "Exploring 1,750,000 Years into Man's Past." *National Geographic.* 1961. Vol. 120, No. 4:564-89.

————. "Finding the World's Earliest Man." *National Geographic.* 1960. Vol. 118, No. 3:420-36.

Linton, Ralph. *The Tree of Culture.* New York: Knopf, 1961.

Napier, John. "The Locomotor Functions of Hominids." In *Classification and Human Evolution,* ed. by S. L. Washburn. Chicago: Aldine, 1963.

Oakley, Kenneth P. "A Definition of Man." In *Culture and the Evolution of Man* (hereafter cited as *Culture and Evolution*), ed. by M. F. Ashley-Montagu. New York: Oxford University Press, 1962.

————. *Man the Toolmaker.* Chicago: University of Chicago Press, 1959.

————. "On Man's Use of Fire, with Comments on Toolmaking and Hunting." In *Social Life of Early Man,* ed. by S. L. Washburn. Chicago: Aldine, 1961.

Washburn, S. L., and Howell, F. C. "Human Evolution and Culture." In *The Evolution of Man,* ed. by S. Tax. Chicago: University of Chicago Press, 1960.

White, Leslie A. "The Concept of Culture." In *Culture and Evolution*.

Chapter 8: The Human Family

Coon, Carleton S. *The Origin of Races.* New York: Knopf, 1962.

Etkin, William. "Social Behavior and the Evolution of Man's Mental Faculties." In *Culture and the Evolution of Man,* ed. by M. F. Ashley-Montagu. New York: Oxford University Press, 1962.

Goldman, Irving. "Status Rivalry and Cultural Evolution in Polynesia." *American Anthropology.* 1955. Vol. 57:680-97.

Goodall, Jane. "My Life Among Wild Chimpanzees." *National Geographic.* 1963. Vol. 124, No. 2:272-308.

Harlow, Harry F. and Margaret K. "Social Deprivation in Monkeys." *Scientific American.* 1962. Vol. 207, No. 5:136-46.

————. "A Study of Animal Affection." *Natural History Magazine.* 1961. Vol. LXX, No. 10:48-55.

Hediger, Heini P. "The Evolution of Territorial Behavior." In *Social Life of Early Man* (hereafter cited as *Social Life*), ed. by S. L. Washburn. Chicago: Aldine, 1961.

Levi-Strauss, Claude. *Structural Anthropology.* Trans. by C. Jacobsen and B. G. Schoept. New York: Basic Books, 1963.

Lowie, Robert H. *Social Organization.* New York: Rinehart and Company, 1948.

Milne, Lorus J. and Margery. *The Senses of Animals and Men.* New York: Atheneum, 1962

Murdock, George Peter. *Social Structure*. New York: Macmillan, 1949.

Reynolds, Vernon. "The Old Man of the Woods." *Natural History Magazine*. 1964. Vol. LXXIII, No. 1:44-50.

Sahlins, Marshall D. "The Origin of Society." *Scientific American*. 1960. Vol. 203, No. 1:77-86.

Schaller, George B. *The Mountain Gorilla: Ecology and Behavior*. Chicago: University of Chicago Press, 1963.

Washburn, S. L., and Devore, Irven. "Baboon Ecology and Human Evolution." In *African Ecology and Human Evolution,* ed. by F. C. Howell and F. Bourlière. Chicago: Aldine, 1963.

————. "Social Behavior of Baboons and Early Man." In *Social Life*.

Chapter 9: Language

Bryan, Alan Lyle. "The Essential Morphological Basis for Human Culture." *Current Anthropology*. June 1963. Pp. 297-305.

Carroll, John B., ed. *Language, Thought, and Reality: Selected Writings of Benjamin Lee Whorf*. New York: Technological Press of Massachusetts Institute of Technology and John Wiley, 1956.

Eiseley, Loren. *"Fossil Man and Human Evolution."* In *Culture and the Evolution of Man* (hereafter cited as *Culture and Evolution*), ed. by M. F. Ashley-Montagu. New York: Oxford University Press, 1962.

Etkin, William. "Social Behavior and the Evolution of Man's Mental Faculties." In *Culture and Evolution*.

Hockett, Charles D. "The Origin of Speech." *Scientific American*. 1960. Vol. 203, No. 3:88-112.

Hoijer, Harry. "The Relation of Language to Culture." In *Anthropology Today,* ed. by O. Kroeber, et al. Chicago: University of Chicago Press, 1953.

Hughes, John P. *An Introduction to Linguistics*. New York: Random House, 1962.

Junod, Henri A. *The Life of a South African Tribe*. New Hyde Park, N.Y.: University Books, 1962.

Pei, Mario. *The Story of Language*. New York: Mentor Books, 1949.

Sapir, Edward. *Culture, Language, and Personality*. Berkeley: University of California Press, 1958.

————. *Language*. New York: Harvest Books, 1949.

Swadesh, Morris. "Linguistics as an Instrument of Pre-History." *Southwest Journal of Anthropology*. 1959. Vol. 15: 20-35.

White, Leslie A. "The Concept of Culture." In *Culture and Evolution*.

Chapter 10: Clothing and Shelter

Coon, Carleton S. *The Origin of Races*. New York: Knopf, 1962.

Darwin, Charles. *The Voyage of H.M.S. Beagle*. New York: The Heritage Press, 1957.

Goodall, Jane. "My Life Among Wild Chimpanzees." *National Geographic*. 1963. Vol. 124, No. 2:272-308.

Hediger, Heini P. "The Evolution of Territorial Behavior" In *Social Life of Early Man*, ed. by S. L. Washburn. Chicago: Aldine, 1961.

Kenyon, Kathleen. "Ancient Jericho." *Scientific American*. April 1954. Vol. 190, No. 4:76-82.

Leakey, L. S. B. "Adventures in the Search for Man." *National Geographic*. 1963. Vol. 123, No. 1:132-52 .

Linton, Ralph. *The Tree of Culture*. New York: Knopf, 1961.

Mellaart, James. "The Beginning of Village and Urban Life." In *The Dawn of Civilization*, ed. by S. Piggott. New York: McGraw-Hill, 1961.

Schaller, George B. *The Mountain Gorilla: Ecology and Behavior*. Chicago: University of Chicago Press, 1963.

Wissler, Clark. *North American Indians of the Plains*. New York: American Museum of Natural History, 1941.

Woolley, Leonard. "From Reed Hut to Brick Palace." *History*. 1959. Vol. 1, No. 1:6-19.

Woolley, Leonard, and Hawkes, Jacquetta. *Prehistory and the Beginnings of Civilization*. New York: Harper and Row, 1963.

Chapter 11: Religion

Breuil, Abbé H. *Four Hundred Centuries of Cave Art*. Montignac, France: Centre d'études et de documentation préhistorique, 1952.

Campbell, Joseph. *The Masks of God: Occidental Mythology*. New York: The Viking Press, Inc., 1964.

————. *The Masks of God: Oriental Mythology*. New York: The Viking Press, Inc., 1962.

————. *The Masks of God: Primitive Mythology*. New York: The Viking Press, Inc., 1959.

Durkheim, Emile. *The Elementary Forms of the Religious Life.* Trans. by J. Swain. New York: Collier Books, 1961.

Goldman, Irving. "Status Rivalry and Cultural Evolution in Polynesia." *American Anthropology.* 1955. Vol. 57:680-97.

Howells, W. W. *The Heathens, Primitive Man and His Religions.* Garden City, N.Y.: Doubleday, 1948.

Hoyle, Fred. *The Nature of the Universe.* New York: Harper and Brothers, 1950.

Maringer, Johannes. *The Gods of Prehistoric Man.* Trans. by Mary Ilford. New York: Knopf, 1960.

Troyer, Johannes. *The Cross as Symbol and Ornament.* Philadelphia: Westminster Press, 1961.

Van Gennep, Arnold. *The Rites of Passage.* Chicago: University of Chicago Press, 1960.

White, Leslie A. "The Concept of Culture." In *Culture and the Evolution of Man,* ed. by M. F. Ashley-Montagu. New York: Oxford University Press, 1962.

Chapter 12: Domesticating Plants and Animals

Anati, Emmanuel. *Palestine Before the Hebrews.* New York: Knopf, 1963.

Bates, Marston. *Man in Nature.* Englewood Cliffs, N.J.: Prentice-Hall, 1961.

Braidwood, Robert J. "The Agricultural Revolution." *Scientific American.* 1960. Vol. 203, No. 3:130-53.

Braidwood, Robert J., and Willey, Gordon R., eds. *Courses Toward Urban Life.* Chicago: Aldine, 1962.

Briggs, Lloyd Cabot. *Tribes of the Sahara.* Cambridge, Mass.: Harvard University Press, 1960.

Childe, Vere Gordon. *The Aryans: A Study of Indo-European Origins.* New York: Knopf, 1926.

Collier, John. *Indians of the Americas.* New York: Mentor Books, 1947.

Dyson-Hudson, Rada. "Men, Women, and Work in a Pastoral Society." *Natural History Magazine.* 1960. Vol. LXIX, No. 10.

Fairservis, Walter A., Jr. *The Ancient Kingdoms of the Nile.* New York: Crowell, 1962.

Lhote, Henri. *The Search for the Tassili Frescoes.* New York: Dutton, 1959.

Linton, Ralph. *The Tree of Culture,* New York: Knopf, 1961.

Murdock, George Peter. *Africa: Its People and Their Culture History*. New York: McGraw-Hill, 1959.

Oakley, Kenneth P. "A Definition of Man." In *Culture and the Evolution of Man,* ed. by M. F. Ashley-Montagu. New York: Oxford University Press, 1962.

Sauer, Carl O. "Sedentary and Mobile Bents in Early Societies." In *Social Life of Early Man,* ed. by S. L. Washburn. Chicago: Aldine, 1961.

Woolley, Leonard, and Hawkes, Jacquetta. *Prehistory and the Beginnings of Civilization*. New York: Harper and Row, 1963.

Chapter 13: Metals Replace Rocks

Bibby, Geoffrey. "Before the Argo." *Horizon*. 1961. Vol. II, No. 6.

Childe, Vere Gordon. *Man Makes Himself*. New York: New American Library, 1951.

Guggenheim, Hans. "Smiths of the Sudan." *Natural History Magazine*. 1961, Vol. LXX, No. 5:8-20.

Linton, Ralph. *The Tree of Culture*. New York: Knopf, 1961.

Mellaart, James. "Roots in the Soil." In *The Dawn of Civilization,* ed. by S. Piggott. New York: McGraw-Hill, 1961.

Singer, Charles. *A History of Technology*. Oxford: The Clarendon Press, 1955.

Woolley, Leonard, and Hawkes, Jacquetta. *Prehistory and the Beginnings of Civilization*. New York: Harper and Row, 1963.

Zim, Herbert S., and Shaffer, Paul R. *Rocks and Minerals*. New York: Simon and Schuster, 1957.

Chapter 14: Writing

Chadwick, John. "The Decipherment of Linear B." *Natural History Magazine*. 1961. Vol. LXX, No. 3:9-19.

Chiera, Walter. *They Wrote on Clay*. Chicago: University of Chicago Press, 1938.

Childe, Vere Gordon. *Man Makes Himself*. New York: New American Library, 1951.

Culican, William. "The First Merchant Venturers: The Sea People of the Levant." In *The Dawn of Civilization* (hereafter cited as *Dawn of Civilization*), ed. by S. Piggott. New York: McGraw-Hill, 1961.

Diringer, David. *The Alphabet*. New York: Philosophical Library, 1948.

————. *Writing*. New York: Praeger, 1962.

Doblhofer, Ernst. *Voices in Stone*. Trans. by Mervyn Savill. New York: The Viking Press, Inc., 1957.

Friedrich, Johannes. *Extinct Languages*. New York: Philosophical Library, 1957.

Gardiner, Alan Henderson. *Egyptian Grammar*. Oxford: The Clarendon Press, 1927.

Linton, Ralph. *The Tree of Culture*. New York: Knopf, 1961.

Mallowan, M. E. "The Birth of Written History." In *Dawn of Civilization*.

Moorhouse, A. C. *The Triumph of the Alphabet*. New York: Harry Schuman, 1953.

Ogg, Oscar. *The Twenty-Six Letters*. New York: Crowell, 1948.

Chapter 15: Civilization

Adams, Robert M. "The Origin of Cities." *Scientific American*. 1960. Vol. 203, No. 3:153-73.

Braidwood, Robert J., and Willey, Gordon R., eds. *Courses Toward Urban Life*. Chicago: Aldine, 1962.

Campbell, Joseph. *The Masks of God: Oriental Mythology*. New York: The Viking Press, Inc., 1962.

————. *The Masks of God: Primitive Mythology*. New York: The Viking Press, Inc., 1959.

Childe, Vere Gordon. *Man Makes Himself*. New York: New American Library, 1951.

————. *What Happened in History*. New York: Pelican Books, 1943.

Kramer, Samuel Noah. *History Begins at Sumer*. Garden City, N.Y.: Doubleday, 1959.

Linton, Ralph. *The Tree of Culture*. New York: Knopf, 1961.

Mallowan, M. E. "The Birth of Written History." In *The Dawn of Civilization* (hereafter cited as *Dawn of Civilization*), ed. by S. Piggott. New York: McGraw-Hill, 1961.

Mellaart, James. "Roots in the Soil." In *Dawn of Civilization*.

Mumford, Lewis. *The City in History*. New York: Harcourt, Brace, and World, 1961.

Woolley, Leonard, and Hawkes, Jacquette. *Prehistory and the Beginnings of Civilization*. New York: Harper and Row, 1963.

SOURCES FOR ILLUSTRATIONS

Page	Source
23	Based on photographs in A. S. Romer's *Man and the Vertebrates*.
25	Ape skeleton after E. Hooton; human skeleton after W. W. Howells.
27	Redrawn from Gustav Schenk's *History of Man*.
30	Adapted from W. W. Howells and Le Gros Clark.
32	After A. S. Romer.
37	After A. S. Romer and Le Gros Clark.
40	Dryopithecine molar pattern after G. G. Simpson.
48	Based on a drawing in François Bourlière's *Natural History of Mammals*.
51	After E. H. Colbert.
52, 53	Based on paintings by Charles R. Knight in the Field Museum.
55	After E. H. Colbert and an exhibit at the American Museum of Natural History.
56	Based on paintings by Charles R. Knight in the Field Museum.
57	After E. H. Colbert.
64	Based on a painting by Z. Burian.
66	Adapted from a skeletal reconstruction by J. Z. Young.
68	Based on paintings by Z. Burian.
69	Adapted from E. H. Colbert, A. S. Romer, and J. Z. Young.

70	Based on a painting by Charles R. Knight in the Field Museum.
72	Based on a painting by Z. Burian.
74	Based on a photograph by Baron Hugo van Lawick in *National Geographic,* February, 1963.
75	After E. Hooton.
78, 79	Based on paintings by Z. Burian.
80	After a reconstruction by J. H. McGregor.
82	Left view: after a painting by P. Bianchi for *National Geographic;* right view: after a reconstruction in the British Museum of Natural History.
84	After W. W. Howells.
85, 87	Based on a painting by Z. Burian.
88–112	Most of the drawings on these pages are composites of several reconstructions: *Plesiadapsis* is after E. L. Simons; *Proconsul* and Rhodesian Man are based on Maurice Wilson's paintings; *Australopithecus africanus* is after the reconstruction by G. E. Smith and A. Forestier.
114	Based on a painting by Z. Burian.
116	Redrawn from a photograph by Baron Hugo van Lawick in *National Geographic,* February, 1963.
118	After W. E. Scheele.
120	Chopper tool after K. P. Oakley; pebble tool after L. S. B. Leakey.
121	Fist ax after W. W. Howells; Acheulian ax after L. S. B. Leakey.
122	After W. W. Howells.
127	Adapted from a photograph by Elspeth Siegrist in Fine Arts Exhibit IV, Metropolitan Museum of Art.
129	Based on a photograph by Fritz Goro for *The Epic of Man* © 1961, Time, Inc.
138	Based on a photograph of the Hall of the Bulls in the Lascaux Cave in France.
145	Based on a photograph by Dr. Donald Thompson in LIFE magazine © 1958, Time, Inc.
150	Based on a painting by Z. Burian.
153	Adapted from a photograph of a Spanish rock drawing.
171	Drawn from a photograph of a statuette by Walter Sanders, Department of Antiquities, Egypt.
174	Based on a painting by Z. Burian.

177   The figure of Adad is part of a stele in the Louvre.
179   The Thoth statuette is in the Louvre.
183   After L. S. B. Leakey.
185   Based on a photograph of a Spanish rock drawing.
195   Drawn from a photograph by Henri Lhote.
204   Drawn from a photograph of a relief in Queen Hatshepsut's temple, Deir el-Bahri.
206   Drawn from a photograph of the Battle Standard of Ur.
210   Based on a photograph of a Spanish rock drawing.
214   Drawn from photographs, Department of Antiquities, Ashmolean Museum, Oxford.
215   Idea-signs after J. Friedrich; stylization after A. C. Moorhouse.
216   The Nar-Mer Palette is in the Cairo Museum.
219   After S. N. Kramer.
227   After D. Diringer and W. Culican.
228   After a reconstruction by Andrade.
233   After a reconstruction by H. D. Darby.

INDEX

DATE DUE